THE RED I

Ben Peek is the author of *The Godless*, *Leviathan's Blood*, *The Eternal Kingdom*, *Above/Below*, *Twenty-Six Lies/One Truth*, *Black Sheep*, and *Dead Americans and Other Stories*. He is also the creator of the psychogeographical 'zine, *The Urban Sprawl Project*, and the autobiographical comic, *Nowhere Near Savannah*. He lives in Sydney, Australia, with his partner and two cats.

BEN PEEK

THE RED LABYRINTH

THIS IS A SNUGGLY BOOK

Copyright © 2025 by Ben Peek.
All rights reserved.

ISBN: 978-1-64525-168-2

For Nik

THE RED
LABYRINTH

'...they contain the tombs of the kings who built the labyrinth, and also the tombs of the sacred crocodiles.'

—Herodotus, *The Histories*

1

ZOJA ROSE never wanted to go to the red labyrinth. Those who say otherwise, the monks and the soldiers who come here and stand in front of you and say it was what Zoja wanted, lie to you when they do. They're nothing but slavers anyway. That's why they're here. They want to put you in chains. They want to sell you so they can raise armies for the Black Queen. They want you to think Zoja is your enemy. She's a dissident, they say. A revolutionary. That's true, at least. But Zoja doesn't care if you believe what the monks tell you, or if you think the soldiers will help you and your families. She doesn't care if you believe in gods or not. I know this because I know Zoja Rose. I know what she cares about and what she doesn't.

Zoja lived in the Red King's kingdom when she was young, lived in this city here, in fact. She lived in one of the narrow streets near the harbour, back when the city was rich with trade and it sprawled darkly and brilliantly over the hills. Zoja lived in a loft above a wig shop. The shop had a red door, just as all the doors in the Red King's city were once red. The colour was a little faded, but the inside of the shop was clean and cramped with wooden isles and racks of waiting hair. The wigs were well made. Zoja sold her creations in the markets on the other side of the city, the markets that have since been torn down and outlawed. She didn't make much money from her wigs, but that didn't matter to her. Zoja's world was a small one and she lived quietly within it and within herself. She lived primarily within her thoughts and within her dreams. She curated her fantasies carefully and built them extensively for she knew that despite the riches around her, success and wealth would not be hers. Zoja was a slim woman, about five foot four, maybe five foot five, with pale skin and blonde hair. Her hair wasn't always blonde, as she sometimes dyed it black or red, but she kept it short and unremarkable so that she could showcase the wigs she made. She was, in truth, a plain young woman, someone you could easily forget at twenty-three, though not at thirty-four.

A lover once asked Zoja why she didn't sell her business. Or at least, he said, look for work in one of the large salons. The two of them were lying in Zoja's bed. It overlooked the poor quarters of the city with a gaze that lingered on the uneven, faded roofs and the broken skyline that led to harbour. Zoja had lit the room with candles earlier in the year, but they'd burnt low over the last month. The light they offered now wasn't strong enough to fully remove the shadows that fell across their bodies. In that light, Zoja often let questions go unanswered. Her lover repeated himself and she thought about ignoring him, or lying.

'This is all I have left of my family,' she said, instead. 'My aunt owned this building before my mother, before me. It was all she had and all my mother had. If I gave it up, I would be giving up them.'

'What do you mean, give it up?' he said. 'You can read and write. You've been educated. You can have more than this.'

'No, I can't. I was never given an education. The Red King's Council never allowed me that. My father died when I was young. He was a builder. He died while working on a site. My mother was a maid. After my father's death, she had to take me to work with her. We'd moved to a small town so that my father could get work. We didn't know anyone who could help us after he died, and my mother couldn't afford to leave me with someone. The family she worked for didn't complain at first. My mother arrived early, before their children went to school, and I would help her prepare their lunches. When their children came back from school I would help them with their chores. After a while the children started to teach me how to read. They thought school was a game and they wanted to share it with me. The three of us went on like that for nearly half a year until their parents found out and put a stop to it. They told my mother that they weren't paying for my education. They were paying her to work, that was all. They fired her because they didn't want to be fined over my unsanctioned education, or have to continue paying for it. After that, my mother was forced to come here, to this city, to where her sister lived. My aunt owned this shop. I was left with her and her husband while my mother went to work. My uncle didn't like me, but my aunt loved me. She taught me all she knew.'

Zoja's lover was a man who called himself Ozias Máutr. It wasn't his real name, Zoja knew. Ozias was a tall man, just over six foot. He had a black beard that'd grown unkempt but not unattractively so. He worked as a barman. Before he'd come to the city, he told her, he had worked in a quarry, and on a snail farm. He was an orphan. The last, Zoja knew, was at least true. His left arm, hip, leg, and much of the left side of his left chest, was covered in an intricate black tattoo much like a spiderweb. It was not the organised web of an orb weaver, not elegant or beautiful, but a tangled one that went this way and that. Every strand of it connected to another in such a chaotic nature that it was impossible for the eye to follow one line to another, much less determine the beginning or end of it.

'The black monks raised me,' he told her earlier, told her one night after they'd first met, after they had gone back to his barren bedsit and she'd seen his tattoos. 'They raise a lot of children. They raise them in the Black Queen's name. People don't often think about them doing that. They think they guard the labyrinth and sit on councils and speak for the queen. They don't see the schools, or the dormitories full of children. Every child they raise is a monk of the labyrinth no matter where they go in this world.'

Zoja had seen labyrinth tattoos before, but never one as large or as intricate as Ozias'. She was mostly familiar with the tattoos of the local monks, the Red

King's monks. They used red ink and put them on the right-hand side of their body. Some of these tattoos were nothing more than single lines. Others ran up to the elbow, or came down from the shoulder. Zoja didn't ask Ozias why his was so much more than those others she had seen. She didn't know the answer, but she had no time for the myths that crept around the neighbourhood about it. Those myths claimed that Ozias had mapped the black labyrinth and escaped, that he had once been the Black Queen's prisoner, that he was a murderer and worse and had been sent to the very depths of the labyrinth. In the most wild stories they told they said he'd lived in the black labyrinth for a thousand years.

Zoja didn't ask him why he had left the monks. She didn't need to. Her aunt had been sentenced to the red labyrinth after she poisoned her husband. The murder had been one of self-defence, but it didn't matter. The Red King's Council sent all who came before it to the red labyrinth, sent them to be judged by the Red King himself, no matter if they were poisoners or philosophers or prostitutes. Her aunt was taken there by two monks. On the morning that they led her aunt out of the jail half a dozen people waited around the cart to say goodbye. They were neighbours and friends. One woman bought a dog who whined the entire time. Zoja's aunt would be driven through the streets of the city before everyone woke, would be taken through the dark lanes that went past the narrow alleys and skeletal parks. She would be taken out into pale, winter-touched hills and up to the local monastery. The silent monks watched as people hugged her aunt, waiting patiently. Zoja hugged her last. Her aunt held her and talked to her mother while she did. She left her sister the shop she owned, left it for her and Zoja. Her aunt's breath was stale, like nothing was alive in her, and the words sounded like someone else's. Once she finished talking, the monks chained her to the floor of their cart and set out.

The world is full of cruelties. Why, Zoja asked herself, would you willingly be part of one? It seemed to her that the most natural thing in life was to want to be free of the monks and the labyrinth, no matter if it was red or black, just as she wanted to be free of the Red King and his suffocating laws. It must not have been easy for Ozias to have left the black labyrinth. Zoja could trace the traumas he'd experienced on his skin, could run her fingers along the scars that merged with the tattoos. They diverged in places, but they never truly left each other. One day, she knew, Ozias would tell her about his life with the Black Queen, but until then she was willing to wait. The realisation surprised her. She had been in love before, but she'd always kept a part of herself separate. She had never told a man before she could read, or that she owned books. She'd never shown them to him, or read from them because he could not. She was twenty-two. He was thirty-four. At night, when she was alone, she worried she'd given him too much of herself.

That spring the rent went up on Zoja's small stall in the markets. She had no choice but to pay, but because of the cost she no longer rode on wagons or in carts.

She was forced to make the trip across the city on foot. If the weather was good, it took her two hours each way. If the weather was bad, if it rained and the streets flooded, Zoja was forced to stay the night in one of the public houses. She would suffer the storms in the morning, but not at night, not when the lamps went out and the roads were dark and flooded. She shared a room with other stall owners, usually five or six of them, and they spread out across the floor. The storms that spring were worse than any you've seen recently. A series of dark fronts washed over the city so violently that Zoja was forced to spend a week in a public house, and would have spent another if the council hadn't closed the markets. According to the issues that were read out, the markets would be closed for a week, maybe more if the weather did not change.

Zoja made her way home in the rain. On the way back, she visited her mother's grave. The trees were pale, broken things throughout the cemetery, and the paths were muddy. Zoja's mother had been dead for four years by then. All the way there Zoja had a terrible premonition. She'd had it since she had awoken, but when she reached her mother's gravestone, she found nothing amiss. Zoja cleaned the stone. She thought about replacing it, thought about ordering something larger that wasn't in danger of being washed away, though she didn't have the money. She huddled beneath her sagging umbrella. She still felt apprehensive. Maybe she should have a gravestone made for her aunt as well. It seemed like a more appropriate spending of the funds she didn't have, even if it was forbidden.

After she left the graveyard Zoja stopped at the public house Ozias worked in. He wasn't there. The building was mostly empty. Vincent, one of the bartenders she knew, waved her over. Quietly, he told her that the prefects had picked up Ozias earlier that morning. The prefects had come in the early hours of the morning, when the rain had been at its worse. Ozias hadn't been surprised to see them, Vincent said. Vincent had just started work himself. He was close enough to hear the prefects ask Ozias questions. At first, Ozias had been polite, even friendly. The prefects asked him how long he'd been in the city, where he lived, and where he'd come from originally. Ozias had been asked those questions before, Zoja knew. He had answers for them, answers that pleased everyone. But, according to Vincent, all that changed when a monk came into the bar. He was a tall, lean man with a red tattoo on his neck. When Ozias saw him, he went still. When the man spoke, Ozias attacked him.

Vincent didn't know what the monk said. He'd spoken in the monk's own language, the language of the labyrinths. But he knew, like everyone did, that monks hunted their wayward brethren and that now there was a monk here for Ozias, a monk who Ozias almost killed in response. It took four prefects to subdue him. Vincent couldn't believe it himself, but Zoja could. She half listened to him while he spoke, while he offered up reasons and explanations. Anyone could have come up with them, Zoja knew. They weren't particularly insightful. She found herself thinking about how she'd woken up earlier and the apprehension she had felt.

She left Vincent and made her way home. She passed an elderly woman selling paper flowers on the street, selling them beneath a sagging umbrella. The woman smiled at her. Zoja smiled back politely, but distractedly. She wanted to help Ozias but knew she couldn't. She wanted to go to the prefect station and ask after him, but it would be foolish to do so. She wanted to ask after him. She wanted to ask someone to help her. There was no one who would, but she wanted someone who would help her because she was powerless. She was so lost in her thoughts that she didn't notice the door to her shop as she approached it, didn't see that it was open. She didn't see the shadows of the prefects inside. She certainly didn't see the prefect in his black and red uniform who appeared on the street next to her. One moment he wasn't there, then he was, his hand holding her arm firmly. His face was narrow, but not sharp. He called her miss, spoke to her politely. He led her inside, led her past the half a dozen prefects in her isles. They watched her pass, standing between the backs of coloured wigs.

The stairs to her loft were still and narrow. The prefect held her, helped her get up when she stumbled at the end, before the door. Two prefects were inside her loft. A monk was there as well. He was bald and had cuts around his head and a split lip. A red tattoo ran thickly from the right side of his body and around half his neck, as if it were a broken collar.

The monk was sitting on the floor at the back of the room. He was reading one of her books. It was a history book about the labyrinths, about how the Red King and the Black Queen made both the red and black labyrinths. It was not typeset but handwritten. It was not her handwriting, but there was another nearly finished volume that was in her hand. Zoja had been copying it over the last two months, a few pages each night. The monk looked up at her as she came in, but said nothing. The prefect sat Zoja on her bed. The other two prefects continued to go through her draws, her clothes, her life.

Finally, the monk came over to her. The book was still in his hand, a finger splitting the pages. The other books, the ones that taught her languages, that spoke about politics, that were references for herbs and medicine, were piled on the floor. They were piled around the false bottom of the dresser she'd hidden them in. 'It is enough of a crime that you read these things,' he said to her. 'But to copy this one, to make a new edition?'

'It is forbidden,' she said, unable to say anything else. 'I know.'

2

ZOJA was taken to a small station down by the harbour. She was marched through the streets by the narrow-faced prefect and two others, her wrists bound but with an umbrella held over her head politely. Her cell was at the back of the station, through two sets of doors with solid locks and bars. The cell itself was a damp cube, the last in two rows of three. It had a small window that leaked rain. The door to the cell had recently been painted a fresh red and the smell lingered with the dampness unpleasantly, like a rot that had just taken.

There were two other prisoners in the cells. The closest to Zoja was a heavyset man who paced around his cell and talked to himself for much of the morning. Zoja sat on her hard cot and listened for a while. He was drunk and his conversation was a litany of self-pity for his situation. It echoed how Zoja felt. The man muttered to himself about his failure to control himself, about the mistakes he'd made, and how he deserved his fate.

The second prisoner didn't speak until after the first was released. The first left late that very same afternoon. He was released during a lull in the rain. The prefect who came to the cell spoke patiently with the man about his drinking and urged him to get help. You're destroying not just yourself, but your family, he said. Only tragedy will come if you continue like this. Zoja wondered if he would say that to her later, but when the same prefect returned with a bowl of soup and a cup of water for her dinner, he said nothing. He placed the meal on the damp floor. The rain had returned by then and the wall was weeping onto the edge of her cot and onto the floor. Zoja thought the prefect might say something about that, might offer her an apology, or move her, but he didn't. He simply closed the cell door. A moment later, he opened another door and repeated the process.

'You're for the red labyrinth,' the second prisoner said after the prefect had left, after the door leading to the six cells was closed and locked.

'No one has said that to me.' Zoja held the warm bowl in her hands. She'd not been given a spoon. 'No one has said anything to me.'

'The prefects will only talk to petty thieves and drunks. For those like you and I, they say nothing.'

'Then you're for the red labyrinth as well?'

'I'm afraid so.'

She sipped her soup. Her hands shook as she did. She had to use both to raise the dented bowl to her mouth. 'How long will we stay here?'

'Until the monks come. Tomorrow, or the next day, I guess. They come to small stations once a week. I've been here five days now.'

Zoja's aunt had waited three days.

'My name is Jacek,' the prisoner said after she didn't reply. 'I was a soldier. I suppose I still am. I was a scout and now I'm a deserter. I was caught trying to get onto a ship here in the harbour. I wanted to buy my way somewhere else.

'I should never have come here. I know that. I know they watch the ships here. But they watch the ships everywhere. Every dock, every port, every coastline of this forsaken country. I just thought I could slip through here. There's a lot of people here. I thought no one would notice me in a crowd. It sounds foolish, I know, but I thought that. I wanted to leave. I had to leave. I couldn't stay. You don't know what's happening out there. The Red King's Council tells you there is a war, but it's no war you can imagine. The Black Queen has lost her throne, they say. The generals tell us soldiers the same thing. They say our freedom is at stake. The majors say it as well, and the captains and everyone else who has a piece of command. You're going to restore order. You're going to help a god. Some of us believed it at first.

'A few days across the border we came across a camp. We hadn't seen anyone until then, just some crows and some wolves out on the edges. The camp we came to didn't have any defences, didn't have any guards, or walls, or anything like that. It was a refugee camp. We walked into it and found everyone dead.

No one had been spared, no matter how old or young they were. They'd been cut up, crushed, and broken. It seemed like just about every manner of brutality had been done to them. It was just them, though. There was no sign of another army. There was no fallen enemy. No bit of broken armour, or a lost weapon. There weren't even tracks. It was like nothing I'd ever seen. I got a chill standing there. I waited for someone to give us orders to clean up the dead, but no one gave that order. We left them for the carrion eaters.

'We came to the Black Queen's cities as we went further on. They were ruined. We passed dead farmers, soldiers, all kinds basically, but the ones that surprised me the most were the monks. They'd been hanged on the side of a road, or from a building roof, or a tree. Sometimes they'd been dragged to impossible heights. Outside the cities we found the fields and orchards, but nothing was growing in them. Some were smouldering, waiting for new fuel. I don't know how, but they were. One field was full of scorched bones, all of them piled high. There must have been four, five hundred bodies there.

'Eventually we came to some heavily fortified compounds. The soldiers in them looked like they'd been fighting for decades, they were that scarred and flat-eyed. They were led by black monks, monks with black labyrinth tattoos, I mean. They told us that the Black Queen's Council was dead and that they had taken command. They told us about warlords rising up against the Black Queen and council members being murdered in their homes. It didn't sound right but it was all you heard that made sense, all that could explain what I'd already seen. There were some rumours, but they were strange things about cities being found in the ground or rising up and didn't make a lot of sense. All I knew was that everyone I met was afraid of what was out there and we were going to be sent out to hunt down those responsible for that fear.

'I was happy to go. At first, I mean. We were all happy to go. After all we'd seen, we wanted to fight the renegade armies, wanted to kill the soldiers who'd brought so much destruction. You don't get to do that much as a soldier. You rarely get to look at an enemy and think that they should die. We believed we would bring peace. We believed it until we discovered that some of the hardest of the Black Queen's soldiers made up the enemy. We believed it until we saw their leader, a woman who wore a crown of wasps and whose feet burned the ground they touched. I know how it sounds, but I saw her once. I was out scouting. A handful of us had been sent out to map a position. I still thought we could defeat the enemy. I thought it had a command we could strike. But then I saw her. I was never more terrified of anything than when I saw her.

'I don't know why I am telling you this. I should stop. You haven't even told me your name. It's just, it's just that I can't stop. I can't stop thinking about what I saw. I can't stop thinking about her. She was awful. She was beautiful. I fled during the night rather than see her again. Five of us refused to go back to our camps. Only one of us wouldn't leave and we killed him even though he promised not to report us so we had time to get away. We agreed to split up after, to go our separate ways because we thought we'd have a better chance of survival. At least that's what I said when I suggested it. But the truth is I said it because I couldn't stand to be with the others, for them to know what a coward I was. I think the others felt the same. But we couldn't fight this. We couldn't fight her. We had no right, we had—'

Jacek stopped, his voice choking on the memories, as if they were real things trying to climb out of him, trying to climb out of a place he'd hidden them in. He whispered an apology to Zoja, before his sobs overtook him.

She said nothing. She wished Ozias was there. She was worried about him. She wanted to know where he was, what was happening to him. She wanted to ask him if what Jacek said was true. She'd heard stories about the war not going well, but not any specific details. She just knew of insignias and ranks coming home, of those being used to tell parents and partners about their dead family. Jacek was the first soldier she'd met. But maybe he wasn't a soldier? Maybe he wasn't a prisoner? She wasn't suspicious, but she was cautious.

She worried that she was the reason the monks found Ozias. She saw Ozias in the bar again, saw him in her mind as the prefect entered and then the monk. She heard them asking questions, but they were not about him like she'd first imagined, or how Vincent said. They were about her. Ozias had always warned her to be careful with her books and her reading and copying, a warning she'd mocked him for because of course she was careful. She knew it was illegal. Besides, she often said, who was she? She was no one. She knew a handful of people, people who weren't connected to anything organised, or militant. She paid for her books by copying them out. She didn't know where the copies went. She wasn't a threat to anyone. She wanted to tell Ozias that again. She was no one, she would say. She would listen to him tease her gently and kindly. She would ask to be hugged. She would ask him about the labyrinths while he held her. She would tell him she was afraid. She took a cold breath in her cell, suddenly aware of where she was. She held her empty bowl in her hands. The rain coming through the window now covered the floor. It seeped out under the door, the only means of escape.

She dreamed of her aunt that night. She was walking through her aunt's shop, the shop she'd first come to nearly fifteen years before. There were no wigs on the shelves, just wooden heads, smooth and featureless. The heads had bothered Zoja when she'd first come to live with her aunt. They had no faces. One morning, before anyone woke, she crept down into the shop and drew eyes and mouths on the heads with a pencil. She couldn't reach them all, just the ones on the lower shelves. In her dream, however, it was not she who took the heads down, but her aunt. Her aunt had them on the floor around her and was drawing faces on them. The faces she drew were in a sequence of distress, with wide eyes and open mouths. Zoja wanted to turn them away, but couldn't. She didn't know why. Her hands wouldn't move towards them. They would only reach out to her aunt, to touch her shoulder, but the other woman didn't respond. Up close, Zoja realised that her aunt's hair wasn't quite right, that it looked like a wig. She reached out to touch the strands, wondering what it was made of, if she should take it off, if this wasn't her aunt. Her fingers reached through the strange hair. They dug through the strands, dug deeper and deeper and never once encountered any resistance. Soon Zoja's hands were completely submerged in her aunt's head but she didn't stop searching and kept reaching in further and further, a feeling of desperation swelling in her as she did, threatening to consume her while her hands turned clawed.

Zoja was woken by the sound of her cell door opening. An old monk stepped inside. He was wrapped heavily in faded red robes. He wore thick leather gloves that had been dyed an ugly red. He waited in the doorway while Zoja got out of bed. He offered her no privacy while she used the bucket at the back of the room. He cuffed her hands after and led her out to where two prefects waited. Zoja didn't recognise either of them. The monk opened another cell. Jacek, it seemed, was already awake. He said something to the monk that she couldn't make out. The monk didn't reply. A moment later, Jacek appeared in the doorway of the cell, his hands cuffed like hers. He was a tall, thin man, his face covered in cuts and bruises that were healing. His hair was the colour of mud and he was unshaven. He was wearing mismatched clothes, stolen clothes, Zoja knew, and most of them too big for him. Only his boots were different. His boots were a soldier's boots, well made and well kept.

He saw her looking at them. 'I couldn't part with them,' he said. 'I should have. They were what gave me away.'

The cart was waiting outside the station. It was larger than the one that had taken her aunt. It was pulled by two oxen. A canvas covering had been put on the back to protect the prisoners from the rain though there was no one inside. Zoja was the first in, Jacek the second. The monk attached them to a heavy chain that ran along the floor, then had them sit opposite to each other. In the next hour another eight people were placed in the wagon and connected to the chain. Zoja waited for Ozias to be led up to the cart, hoped that he would be even as she hoped he wouldn't. He never appeared. The only person she recognised was Nicholas Greene. He was the last prisoner to be led to the cart by the monk. A large prefect accompanied him. He had to lift Nicholas into the back.

Nicholas had been beaten badly. His face, usually round and pleasant, was bruised and cut and disfigured by swelling. He had lost an eye and Zoja thought his jaw was broken. His clothes were torn and covered in dried blood. He breathed heavily through his mouth, a mouth that revealed lost and broken teeth. Zoja had known Nicholas for half a dozen years. He owned a small business in the neighbourhood that delivered meat to butchers and grocers, as well as imported vegetables and spirits. He was small and portly and polite.

He was well liked. Few people knew that he traded books with people like Zoja.

The cart left the city after Nicholas was secured. Zoja couldn't see much of what was around her, but she saw the gates recede and the forest close in. It was enough. Zoja knew where she was going. She knew the old road. It was cobbled in places and dirt in others. It made a long, circuitous journey through hills that turned into mountains, that became imposing, rocky faces. The road wound up and around each of these new features as the sky embraced it. At the end of this road was an entrance to the red labyrinth. Zoja tried to escape the thought but she couldn't. The rain started to come down. It leaked into the cart. Everything smelt wet. It would be the last time Zoja smelt the rain, she thought, the last time she experienced the weather. Ahead of her was a life of tunnels, twisting, endless tunnels, and a darkness that was complete and utter. She would say goodbye to everything she knew within hours, just like I once said goodbye to everything I knew when I was taken to the red labyrinth.

Someone in Zoja's cart began to cry. For a brief moment she thought it was herself, but it wasn't. It was a man further down from her. She didn't know him.

The entrance to the red labyrinth was within a monastery that had been built on a flat part of a hill, before the hill turned into a mountain. Shallow steps led up to the gate and the stone walls. The two oxen pulled the cart under duress. Once they arrived, they were unhitched and taken away by the monks before any came for Zoja and the others. From the back of the cart, she could see a handful of red monks. Some held umbrellas, some did not. Beyond them were wet walls that stood solidly before her and the rest of the world. When she stepped out of the cart, she saw the monastery's gardens and its pens of chickens and pigs and other livestock. The monastery itself spread out in a collection of large, beautiful stone buildings. There were five small towers spread throughout the nearly two dozen buildings. She wondered if in one of these towers was the entrance to the red labyrinth. She didn't know why she thought that. After all, the path to the red labyrinth led downwards, not upwards.

The old monk who had driven the cart was joined by another two months, both of them wrapped in heavy red robes and holding umbrellas. The three of them organised prisoners into a line and led them into the monastery. Zoja was at the front with Jacek. She was taken to a hall full of tables, where more monks waited for them. There, Zoja and the others were stripped and examined. It was a clinical examination, searching for injuries and illness, an examination that was at once deeply invasive and impersonal. The woman who examined Zoja was in her forties and with short salt and pepper hair. She had a small array of red tattoos around her right wrist and forearm. She said nothing to Zoja while she examined her. Once she was finished, she indicated to a pile of clothes next to her, clothes that were meant to replace those Zoja had arrived in. They were solid work clothes, tough and durable and with no dye in them. After Zoja was dressed, the monk directed her to the other side of the room, where the other prisoners had begun to gather.

A voice stopped her halfway there. The monk who had caught her, the one with a tattoo that was like a chain around his neck, spoke to the woman who examined her. He spoke in the monk's language. Zoja didn't understand him, but the meaning was clear. He pointed to Zoja and to Nicholas. The latter was sitting at his examination table, his eyes closed. The monk pointed to a door opposite the one the other prisoners waited at. As Zoja was led there she thought about fleeing, but she didn't. She couldn't, she realised. She thought of all the things she had read. She knew she should flee, but like so many others who had been where she was, she was paralysed by the authority of the monks and the Red King. Like I was, like all of us who stood in a monastery before we were led down to the red labyrinth, Zoja waited because she could not do anything but wait.

3

ZOJA was taken to the smallest tower of the monastery, to the southern tower. She was put in a small, damp cell there.

She was kept there for nine months. Her interrogator was the monk who had come for her. His name was Jan. He introduced himself during their first official meeting, when she was brought down from her cell to Jan's work room, to a circular room full of wooden tables and metal devices Zoja would soon learn to name.

Jan liked to talk. He talked in languages she knew and in languages she did not. He talked about books he'd read and thought she had. He talked about the things he wanted to know about and the things he thought she knew already. Sometimes he talked about life at the monastery. He talked about crops and farm animals. He very rarely left the monastery, he admitted. 'I'm not a fan of cities,' he said. He didn't like the size, or the smell, or the people. The people watched him. They were wary of him. It was because of his tattoos, he knew. He talked about the things in his workshop, about the spiked hoods and screws and knives, about their history in general and their history to him. He kept heads in jars. He told Zoja their names. He told her how many eyes and teeth he had taken over the years. He kept them in jars as well. Jan favoured a psychological approach to his work which is why he talked, why he named his past victims and counted his trophies in front of new ones. When he wasn't talking, he deprived Zoja of sleep, took away her clothes, and refused to give her toiletries. He wouldn't allow her to wash. He starved her. He overfed her. He drugged her. He bombarded her with sound. For the last, he chained her to the floor of his workshop and had a series of young monks stand near her and clash cymbals for hours and hours on end. The sound was agonising. Zoja screamed and cried and pleaded for them to stop. Later, Jan told her that they were deaf. I found them when they were children, he said, and raised them myself. They're my sons and daughters. He talked to them in sign language. After a few months, Zoja began to understand bits and pieces of it, but its full breadth was not something she was in a condition to learn. There were five deaf monks who Jan called his family. One was present when Zoja cut her right little finger off.

 She cut it off in the seventh month of her interrogation though she did not know what month it was. By then, Zoja had lost all sense of self or any notion of time. She no longer counted the days because she could not separate yesterday from last week or last month. On her worst days, she did not even know if it was morning or evening, or night or day. Sometimes, she would look down at herself and wonder whose body this was, or where she was. She started to dream about her mother in her cell and those dreams continued when she was awake. More than once Zoja thought that her body was her mother's. She watched her mother be cremated, but there were no fires. She told Jan that. By then, she'd already told him all she knew. It wasn't much because Zoja was truly no one in the larger sense of the world. Some will say otherwise now, but they don't know. Zoja Rose was no one. She didn't know any of the leadership Jan wanted to know about. She didn't know addresses or meeting times. She didn't know passwords, or codes. She only knew poor Nicholas, who she had not seen since they had been led up into the tower and to different cells. Still, she heard him sometimes screaming and sobbing, just as she heard other prisoners and how they heard her. She told Jan she got her books from Nicholas. She made fresh copies for him. She didn't write her own work, or elaborate on what she read. She didn't teach others how to read, or read for them. The only thing that made her more than nothing was her relationship with Ozias, but Jan refused to talk about him. When Zoja asked about Ozias, when she asked where Ozias was, where he'd been taken, if he was safe and well or otherwise, Jan shrugged. He didn't know anyone by the name of Ozias, he said. Perhaps she meant someone else? If she could give him another name, he might be able to answer the question, but she only knew him by the one name.

'Maybe my mother knows his name,' Zoja said.

'Does your mother talk to you?' Jan asked.

'Sometimes I see my mother talking.'

'What does she tell you?'

'I can't hear her voice. She just stands there on fire and talks. Sometimes I try to put the fire out, but I can't.'

'Do you know what this means?'

'She is the Red King's servant.'

'The Red King owns us all.' Jan spoke to the deaf monk with his hands. Shortly after, the monk appeared beside him with an old, heavy knife. He placed it in front of Zoja. The end of the knife was not pointed, but flat. 'You've seen this before,' Jan said. 'We've talked about it. I told you that once we reached the end of our relationship, the Red King would come for you and ask for a gift. Others have cut out their tongues and removed their eyes for our god. They do it to ask for his mercy. He has sent your mother for you to show you that he is ready for you. So I must ask what it is that you will give him?'

Zoja gave her finger. Later, she realised that she was not answering his question, or bowing before the Red King, but responding to Jan's suggestion, just like all who had been broken by the monk before. And Zoja was broken. She no longer saw within herself a person that should be preserved, or protected. She was no more than rotten pieces that could be broken apart with a simple tool and discarded. She did not cry out when she drove the flat end of the knife into the joint between her little finger and her hand. The pain was there, but it felt like it belonged to someone else.

When Zoja was back in her cell, when the wound had been sealed roughly by the deaf monk, she wondered what she would cut off after she'd cut across the rest of her hand. She would start on her toes, or maybe with an eye. She would need her left hand to cut, after all, and she would have to preserve that.

Fortunately, she was not asked for anything more. Jan lost interest in her. It was as if, with the parting of her finger, with her first act of self-mutilation, she'd finally proven herself to be of no consequence. He still saw her, in part because he was a meticulous man, but he did so less frequently. In the meetings they had he was distant and uninterested. He would ask her about her diet and how her strength was returning. He would sit with her for a handful of minutes before he would stand and motion to one of his silent monks to take her away. It hurt Zoja, but she couldn't explain why. She worried that he was angry with her, or that she'd done something wrong. She tried to invent lies for Jan, lies that would please him, but he would only shake his head when she began to tell them to him.

Jan returned to his old self on Zoja's last visit. At the end of her ninth month of captivity, she was brought down to his chamber by the most silent of silent monks. There, Jan's tools and devices lay on the floor, much like a librarian who had laid out their books to be catalogued and itemised.

'I'll not see this room for a while,' he said once he had invited her to sit, once he had seated himself across from her. 'Perhaps I'll never see it again. The Red King has asked for my expertise elsewhere. He has another prisoner for me, but that prisoner cannot be brought here. I must travel to him.'

Zoja said nothing.

'He was once one of us,' Jan continued. 'Some have said he was the best of us, once upon a time. Perhaps. Perhaps he was, or perhaps he simply showed promise until he abandoned his responsibilities.'

'Are you talking about Ozias? Could you take a message to him for me? Could you tell him I am sorry.'

'I don't know anyone by that name.' His tone changed, reverted to the bored tolerance that had been in place over the last month. 'I've told you this before, Zoja. It's not polite to keep asking about this man who doesn't exist. You only make a nuisance of yourself. You must remember that when you are in the red labyrinth. If you continue to act this way there, you will find life difficult down there.'

4

AN elderly monk came to examine Zoja in her cell. She wasn't sure if a night had passed since she saw Jan, or a week. She supposed it didn't matter. The monk was a small, thin woman with a raw face and swollen, cold fingers. Once the monk finished the examination, she took out a tattooing kit. She scratched a pattern on the inside of Zoja's right wrist with red ink. The pattern was not complex. It was half a dozen lines in length. Afterwards, Zoja lay on her cell floor and stared at the marks as if they were a question she could find answers to.

The elderly monk returned after the tattoos had healed. She was accompanied by two other monks, both of them male, both of them seemingly younger and stronger than the other. Zoja struggled to tell them apart. Their features slipped into one another like they were deformed twins, or broken replicas. They bound her hands with rope. The elderly monk led all three of them out of the stunted tower and into the courtyards and fields of the monastery's grounds. The sky was overcast, but the light hurt Zoja's eyes.

She stared at the path, at the bits of stone and gravel among the mud. Zoja remembered how she'd been when she first arrived at the monastery, how she had tried to savour what she saw of the world because she wouldn't see it again. The memory felt like someone else's now, a stranger who had stolen her body only to abandon it here.

She entered one of the large buildings. It was full of jars and boxes and trays, all neatly stacked and organised. Most of what was present was preserved food, but there were also clothes and bedding and blankets. At the end of the room was a series of empty animal pens. There was a door after the pens, a stone door painted red. Beyond it was a large circular room. There was a large cage and pulley system in the centre above a hole that led into a deep darkness. Zoja thought she would be locked inside the cage by the monks, but they walked to the back of the room instead. A set of lanterns had been hung from the wall there. In the floor was a set of stairs that led downwards, that led into the dark.

The stairs were narrow and steep. They were part of the walls, had been made somehow while the hole was dug. The monks wound the rope from Zoja's waist to their own, chaining all four of them together. A railing was set into the wall, but it stopped abruptly after one level, leaving only the rough wall as a support. The lamps they carried revealed stairs that circled. They turned again and again and Zoja likened them to a series of repeating mouths, the teeth of which had grown unevenly.

A doorway appeared on the stairs. The door was painted red and made from stone, but unlike the earlier one, it was much, much thicker. The door reached up to the flight of stairs above, ensuring that there was no break for someone to climb over or under. It took the strength of both young monks to push the door open, to reveal the stairs that lay behind it. The outer part of the door frame, Zoja saw, was lined with broken glass and the remains of blades. A grip on it was impossible without maiming your hands. The two monks pushed the heavy door back into place once Zoja was through. There was no handle to pull it open.

She wondered how the monks would return before she realised that they would not. She passed through two more doors, unable to understand the thought fully. Why would anyone willingly come here? Why would the monks want to enter the red labyrinth? By now the entrance was well and truly out of sight. Zoja and the monks were descending through the darkness, illuminated by two lonely lanterns. Ahead of her, the elderly monk took the lead and rarely stopped for rest. When she did, she would sit silently on the narrow stairs and wait for her strength to return. The monks had no water, or food with them, despite what lay above. Were they being punished, Zoja wondered? They must be. They must have broken faith with their brethren. But why bring her? Why allow the elderly monk to tattoo the marks of the red labyrinth on her before they left? Zoja closed her eyes. She tried to imagine herself in her cell, in her safe confinement, but couldn't. When she opened her eyes, the darkness was still around her, still threatening to drown her.

The elderly monk rose. They continued down the stairs. Occasionally Zoja stumbled on the narrow steps, but the younger monks were like anchors and she never fell. After a while a chill began to seep into her and her legs began to tremble. Zoja had never felt claustrophobic before, but as she walked around and around in a slow, descending circle, as she passed through more and more heavy doors surrounded by glass and metal, she began to feel increasingly pressed upon. Blood stains began to appear around the doors. Zoja tried to tell herself that it was paint, but she knew it wasn't. How many people had tried to escape by these stairs? she asked. She asked aloud. Her voice echoed dully around her. The monks didn't answer her. They continued to walk. They walked down more stairs, through more doors and past more stains. Soon, the stairs began to look as if they'd been painted with blood.

Finally, they reached the end. Zoja stepped onto a flat surface. A red stone door appeared out of the darkness. It looked like it had been painted onto the wall, but the monks opened it easily and a narrow stone passage followed. The monks extinguished their lanterns and, plunged into a sudden and complete darkness, Zoja could do nothing but allow herself to be pulled along after them. She ran her hands along the rough stone walls to gain some sense of direction and independence and felt the passage turn, first to the left, then to the right and right again before she stumbled down a small flight of stairs. She was not sure if she turned left or right after that and was unable to regain her sense of direction fully. Her only relief came when a light appeared ahead of her. It started as a blurred piece of colour, a burning light in the distance, but grew to reveal the end of the corridor. The monks pressed forward, eager to leave, but Zoja found herself suddenly reluctant, wanting to stop, to return to the darkness and the stained stairs. The light continued to grow like a fire that'd burned low with exhaustion, like it came from a field of smouldering bones.

She stepped out of the corridor and into the red labyrinth reluctantly. At first, because of that trepidation, Zoja didn't realise exactly how strange and othered the world she stepped into was. She was thinking of a world she knew, a world she'd heard about, and could imagine. She saw buildings, not houses, but shops and markets. She saw lamps that lined the roads and formed fuzzy blooms of light that repeated again and again in patterns she couldn't easily decipher. It was by following that light, by trying to understand it, that Zoja realised she was standing in the middle of a giant hollow inside the earth. The hollow was so immense that she couldn't see the edges of it, just endless roads and bridges and paths that ran from all heights and all directions like the most tangled of spider's webs. It divided the area into levels that crossed and turned and lapped each other like some fevered dream where there was no true end or start. Spread throughout the levels were buildings of various size and purpose, each of them intricately designed to be entered and exited from different levels and sides, thus removing any idea of a front or back. The paths ran in loops everywhere except for a sphere that was ahead of her, that sat like a setting moon but was in fact a building. To call it a building, however, was to suggest something that you have seen before, something that your lives had encountered in a world defined by mundane moments and thoughts. The building was a marvel of construction, numbering over a hundred floors. But it was constantly changing and shifting in shape and design as if caught in a dream dreamt by millions and millions of people. The dreamers of this building might well have been standing before Zoja, for what she saw through all this strange architecture was not the people like you or I, but the dead. The dead who were the true citizens of the red labyrinth. If they had numbered but a few, Zoja might have missed them, for the dead were faint and colourless outlines of who they'd once been. They retained the barest detail of their individuality. But the dead were in legion and they could not be ignored. They walked the streets of the red labyrinth, sat at the tables, and talked to each other in silent voices. They flew through the air, as well, and slunk across the tops of buildings and ran through the streets for the dead in the red labyrinth were not just human, but every living creature that had once moved through the world, all of whom were caught in this ghastly world that no one could have ever imagined outside a nightmare.

5

ZOJA'S rope was undone while she stood and watched the dead. A small group of monks came out and met those she'd arrived with, but she ignored them. She already knew what would happen to her. She would be taken away, would be taken to her new cell. The only thing that would be different now would be what the cell was like. Before she'd thought that her cell would be similar to the one she'd been kept in for the last nine months. Now she wasn't so sure. Zoja stood on a road not far from a public house. Its patrons were all dead, but those who were serving them were all alive, she saw. They were all wearing the rough brown clothes she wore. Those like her were working, were cleaning tables, were standing behind the bar, and were bringing out meals and drinks for dead humans and dead animals alike. She watched a woman place a bowl on the ground for a group of dogs while a man placed a tray of drinks on a table. The dead could not eat or drink what was brought to them, but they mimed the act of consumption. It was as if they were part of a performance, were caught in a play where they had to portray themselves when they'd been most pleased, when they'd come to the bar after they'd finished the day's work, or to meet a friend. Zoja saw the scenes of pleasure repeated again and again without joy as she was led through the red labyrinth. She passed dead people who walked their dogs and bought vegetables and flowers on the streets. The vendors stood beneath greasy lamps and sold real vegetables and flowers as if they were in the Red King's city. Once the transaction was complete, the items the dead bought were placed in bags behind the stands.

Zoja walked through narrow streets, across bridges, and down stairs, the dead passing her, the monk forcing her to give way no matter if they were human or not. The number of dead that crowded the streets and buildings was so immense that Zoja felt overwhelmed. Generations and generations of people and creatures echoed the lives they'd once lived with sad, featureless abandon. The attention they paid to the living appeared non-existent and Zoja asked the new monk if the dead saw them truly, but he refused to answer. He was middle aged and grey and balding. She thought he might be mute until he stopped by a pair of monks. These monks had stopped a prisoner on the street and asked to see their tattoos. They had the look of prefects and Zoja thought they were armed beneath their robes.

After the monks finished talking Zoja was delivered to a large dormitory. The doors of the dormitory were painted red, like all the doors she'd passed in the red labyrinth. The inside was full of tiny, square rooms.

An elderly woman showed them to her. She was not a monk, but she ran the dormitory. She was tall and thin and wore rough robes. She had faded tattoos on her right arm. They were more intricate than Zoja's, but only just. Her name, she said after she'd taken charge of Zoja, was Lo. She took Zoja upstairs to assign her a room. She used a cane to navigate the narrow corridors and steep stairwells. The small rooms she showed had two double bunks in them, one on each side of the wall, and a small dresser without a mirror to divide them. There were no doors on any of the rooms. For privacy, a heavy red cloth was used.

I first met Zoja in one of those rooms. In fact, I was one of her roommates. Lo brought her to the room that Emy, Signe and I shared. The rooms were not segregated by gender, but Lo had the habit of putting women with women and men with men when they first arrived. She said it caused less drama. She'd been running the dormitory for over thirty years, so I suppose she knew what was best. She didn't mind if it changed later. She understood that some of us started relationships, made new friends, and fell out with our original roommates. I knew it too. I'd experienced all those things since I'd come to the red labyrinth.

I had lived with Emy and Signe for the last six years. We were all older than Zoja. We were in our late thirties and early forties. We'd come together because we worked in the same restaurant and because we'd settled into a comfortable, shared solitude. Emy was the oldest of us, lean and worn and short-haired. Signe was the shortest and stoutest and youngest. I was forty-one, though I looked the oldest. I had been beautiful once, though. My hair had been thick and dark, not a mix of black and grey splits and tangles like it was then. My skin had been smooth and pale, not scarred and tattooed.

We didn't talk much that first night. I would be lying if I said I saw any sign of what would happen then, or that I had any idea of what was ahead. Zoja looked like any woman who had just come to the red labyrinth. Her hair had been shaved down to her scalp. She was uncomfortably thin. The trip down had exhausted her. She was overwhelmed by everything around her. She shared a bunk with Signe, and was given the top Signe steadfastly refused to take. She was afraid of rolling off at night, or at least that was what she told Zoja. Emy and I knew differently. Our previous roommate had died in bed a week ago and Signe was afraid the woman's ghost would return at night. Emy and I had told Signe that such things didn't happen, but she refused to believe us.

We worked in a restaurant, like I said. It was a few miles from the dormitory. Before we left for our first shift, Zoja asked if her tattoo was really a map because she couldn't see how it applied to the world around her. It was, I said. It was only a small map, only a small set of lines that led from the dormitory (unmarked but at her wrist) to the restaurant (also unmarked but at the opposite end of her tattoo). But her tattoo was more than a map, I explained. It was a description of her new position and her new life. Any monk or prisoner who looked at her markings would know where she belonged and what she did. I showed her my tattoos, showed her the ones on my wrist like hers, and the ones I'd been given on my collarbone when I first arrived. I hadn't always worked at the restaurant, I said. I don't know how it happened, but I was the one who got the job of explaining things to Zoja while Emy and Signe listened.

When we reached the restaurant I showed Zoja the long tables, the cabinets full of scratched plates and cups, the sinks for washing, and the kitchen itself. It was a large kitchen, and at the back was a storeroom full of ingredients. Some of it was fresh, some of it preserved. 'All of the food has been poisoned,' I said while we stood in the doorway and looked at what anyone would have called a bounty. 'When you work with anything here, you have to wear gloves, a mask, goggles, an apron, and tie your hair back. You have to understand, none of the food here is for us. It's all for the dead. We will prepare it and serve it for them. They will come and sit at the tables and eat it, except of course they won't because they can't. After they've finished, you'll collect the meals and throw it out. It's a hard job, sometimes, because the food here is better than anything you'll eat back at the dormitory. You will be tempted every day to take from the tables, but you mustn't.'

It wasn't until Zoja was delivering food, until she was standing in the long dining room full of dimly-lit tables, until she was looking at the meals she'd place down and watching the dead eat without actually eating, that she understood my warning in full. It wasn't only the dead who sat down to eat, she learned, but dead who had also once served. The prisoners who had died while working for the restaurant continued to work at it. They continued to set tables just as they did when they were alive, continued to serve food, pour drinks, and clean afterwards, all without being able to touch or interact with a single thing.

'It's the same everywhere in the red labyrinth,' I said. We were in the kitchen then, washing dishes. It was at the end of Zoja's first shift. There were a dozen prisoners with us, each of them wearing gloves, goggles, masks and aprons, just as we were. 'It doesn't matter if you're a prisoner in the gardens, or in the public houses, or the stables. Our dead are there. I was sentenced to the Red King's brothel when I first came here. The monks keep all the women there in locked rooms and while you eat better and sleep in better beds, you're raped every night until you're pregnant. The dead come into your rooms while it happens. Sometimes they sit and appear to watch, sometimes they just pass through. When you're pregnant the monks send you to a ward where you stay until you give birth or your pregnancy ends. There are dead doctors wandering through those rooms with the dead nurses, dead pregnant women, and even dead babies. Then, after you give birth, you're sent back to get pregnant again. You never see your children. The monks take them from you at birth. They don't even tell you the gender. They just take them. I had five children while I was there and never saw a single one. I thanked the Red King himself the day they told me I'd never have another child and sent me here.'

We cooked five meals per shift in the restaurant. There were three shifts, each going for nine hours a day, each shift overlapping the other by an hour. The work was physically demanding, but it was the psychological struggle that Zoja truly endured in the first month. I understood it. Most of us suffered like she did. The meals we had in the dormitory were small and plain. You would often arrive at the restaurant hungry and prepare a series of large, communal meals that would go uneaten. There was nothing elaborate about what the prisoners cooked, but we cooked with fresh ingredients and it smelt good. We could have fed every prisoner in the dormitory three times over with what we made each day. But instead, we would take the food down to a large compost and dispose of it there. The compost was regularly cleaned out by the prisoners who worked the waste shifts. They would collect the food and our bodily waste together. None of this helped Zoja, however. She was consumed by the thought of the food she made. She saw it in her dreams. Hunger gnawed at her while she lay in bed. She could almost taste the sauces she mixed, the meat she cooked, the vegetables and fruits she sliced. It was so bad that sometimes she got lost in conversation. We understood, but there wasn't much any of us could do. You had to find your own way to deal with it.

For Zoja, that happened the day she saw her aunt. She saw her as she carried a tray of food down to the end of the restaurant to feed the crowded dead. Zoja had done it before, done it at that spot at that time during the day even, but she hadn't seen her aunt until then.

Sometimes the dead were absent, though no one knew why. We still don't know why. Sometimes they were gone and then they returned. In the case of Zoja's aunt, she appeared during the shift and joined the dead prisoners who cooked meals and carried trays and cleaned the tables, just as Zoja and the other prisoners did.

She was in tears when we came out to find her, in tears after she'd dropped her trays. She asked if any of us had known her aunt.

'She was here for a few years,' I said while I helped Zoja clean up the food. 'She'd killed her husband, people said. I don't know if that's true or not. I didn't know her well. But that's what people said. After a while she moved in with a man. They were private. They lived with another couple. The four of them kept to themselves. Then, one day, your aunt's partner got sick. There's no medicine here if you get sick. No way to help someone who could be helped if you lived outside the red labyrinth. After he died she seemed okay. I talked to her a little. We all did. We wanted to help. We thought she was doing fine. But then, one day, she sat down at the table and ate. There was nothing we could do once she started. We let her finish her meal, then wrapped her body up and took it back to Lo.'

Zoja saw her aunt regularly. She continued to work in the restaurant, continued to mimic the tasks she'd once done, the tasks Zoja now did. One night, Zoja told us that it was not the sight of her aunt that stopped her cravings, but the cruelty. The red labyrinth was a cruel place, she said. 'The cruelty is the point,' I told her quietly.

6

IN the months that followed, Zoja managed her new life as well as she could. She did this by focusing on her work at the restaurant, not because she loved it, or because of any work ethic she had, but because it allowed her to sleep. She was haunted by a slight insomnia and exhaustion was the best aid. Sometimes she drank and sometimes she used, but neither alcohol nor drugs were all that common in our part of the red labyrinth. I could spend a whole night talking to you about how these things were created within the Red King's labyrinth and how they were trafficked, but it's enough to say that as far as everyone in our low, lonely dormitory was concerned, our demands were always unfulfilled.

One day, about four, or five months after Zoja's arrival, a messenger came for her. He was an old, pale monk, one of those monks who was born in the red labyrinth and whose skin bordered on being transparent. He had a series of detailed tattoos that ran up his arm and over his chest. He wore a red robe that showed these tattoos and thus showed us how important he was. He said nothing to us while he stood outside our room. We weren't surprised. Most of the monks like him didn't speak to us. They refused to speak in any of the common languages. It was beneath them, they said. They only spoke the language of the labyrinths. Lo spoke it and she told us what the monk wanted. Zoja had been requested at the death house, she said. She would stay there two nights before she returned.

The death house was where the monks went to die. They let us prisoners die at our jobs, or in the streets, or in our beds, but for themselves, they had rituals and celebrations. Zoja didn't know who would want to see her at the death house, but she went regardless. She didn't have a choice after all. She stood outside the dormitory and looked at the red labyrinth as it swarmed around her, at the dense, intricate network of streets and paths and tunnels that ran through the murky, smoky world that seemingly had no boundaries. It was knowable, she was sure of that, but she would never be given the chance to learn it. She was nothing within the red labyrinth. She was fuel for the dead economy around her. Maybe that's all she had ever been. She'd deceived herself when she had lived in the Red King's city. She had let herself believe that she was an individual, that she was unique, and that she could govern her own life and live how she wished. She couldn't believe she'd lived like that. She could only recount her mistakes as she walked through the tangle of undecipherable paths that the old monk knew.

The death house was a series of simple, elegant cottages potted through a series of large stone gardens.

The design surprised Zoja because it was so different from the commercial design of her cell, of her servitude in a world where the dead lived as if on some eternal, forsaken holiday. She'd not imagined that anywhere in the red labyrinth would be different. Of course, the dead were still there. You could not escape them. They wandered around the cottages, or glided through the air. They were different to those Zoja saw in the restaurant, however. The dead around her were all monks. They walked the quiet paths that weaved through the cottages, sat near the still ponds, or rested in the stone gardens. None of them lingered in the hallways she walked through, or came into the sparse room she was locked in for the night.

She was given breakfast in the morning, but not allowed to leave the room. Music started while she ate. It was sombre, but not sad. Whoever was playing did so for one turn of an hourglass, then stopped. Silence followed. After another turn, someone else began to play. It went like this until the middle of the day when the pale monk returned for her. He said nothing, merely indicated that she should rise and follow him. He led her through a series of quiet halls, then outside and across part of the stone gardens, and finally to a small, solitary cottage that sat beside a still pond.

Inside was another monk, but this monk Zoja knew. It was the monk who'd examined her before she came down to the red labyrinth, the monk who had walked before her down the stairs and through the doors.

The elderly monk looked happy and content. She'd bathed recently and smelt of soap and perfume. She was wearing an elegant red robe that hid her tattoos. The robe itself was beautifully made and as expensive as the tables and chairs throughout the room. The monk had an elaborate platter of food stretched out before her, as well as a bottle of wine and a single glass. 'Please, join me,' she said, indicating to the chair across from her. 'You're welcome to eat, if you wish.'

'I'll pass,' Zoja said. Behind her the door was closed and she and the woman were left alone. 'But thank you.'

The woman laughed a little but there was no humour in it. 'My name is Isa,' she said. 'I've had a few other names over time, names I was given, or that I took, but Isa is my first name, the name the monks gave me as a child. It pleases me to use it, if you don't mind.'

'I didn't know you by any other name.'

There was a thin knife on the table. Isa used it to spread jam over a slice of bread. 'I didn't tell you my name?'

'No.'

'How strange. Are you sure?'

'I'd remember if you had.'

'You weren't well when we met. That's why I had the two younger men come with me. I wanted to make sure you could complete the walk we took, my walk. It's a spiritual journey. I didn't want to ride in the cage. The two men did when they returned to the monastery later but the walk down is a blessing. They'll remember both our names because of it. But I suppose it doesn't matter now. I, at least, remember your name. Zoja. A beautiful name. The Red King had a child by that name. You should be proud of it.'

She wasn't interested in if she should be proud of her name or not. 'Why did you ask for me? The other monk wouldn't explain why I was here.'

'No, he wouldn't. You're here because I asked for you. You were my last task and today is my last day among the living. I go to the Red King's divine reward after this.'

'Because of that you wanted to see me?'

Isa took a bite of her bread. 'Is it so strange?' she asked, her mouth full.

'One of my roommates was once a prostitute. She worked in a brothel in the Red King's city. It still exists. It's very popular. It's very safe. People thought the same about it when my roommate worked there. But it was raided, still. It was raided despite the bribes it paid and the clientele it kept. The women who worked there were charged and sent here. I don't know what happened to the men, but the women who were sent here—'

'Were used. I know the story. I saw the women come here. I've seen other young women come here and be used for the Red King. New monks must have mothers, after all. You should be pleased you avoided that fate.'

'You'll forgive me if I'm not excited to see you, then,' Zoja said. 'You should have requested something else.'

'It was a small request. I only have small requests left. I want to eat the food I loved as a child, I want to drink the wine I have long admired, and I want to sate my curiosity. You are the last of those.'

'What could you possibly want to know?'

'I want to know how you're finding the Red King's Labyrinth. I want to know how you like the taste of his justice?'

'I hate it.'

'No moment of consideration?' Isa smiled and revealed her jam-stained teeth. 'Just an answer, just like that? No pause, no breath.'

'No breath.'

'Good.'

'Good?'

'Yes. At times, I have envied your kind. It's terrible to admit, but it's true. A lot of us who serve outside the red labyrinth do. We serve in the Red King's name. We serve in the Red King's grace. But it is you who serve at his divine side in his divine kingdom. You witness his power every day you are here. You sit in his promise to us all. I worried that you would take pleasure from it.'

'If people saw this...' Zoja paused. She looked around the room. She saw the beauty that was on offer and found that it angered her. 'Do you think there is kindness here for you after you die? There isn't. You'll not live in beauty after you're dead. You'll just be another prisoner in the Red King's labyrinth.'

'Of course you would say that,' Isa said while she sliced a new piece of bread. 'You're a criminal and you cannot see those who are better than you, or the grace they are given.'

She began to reply, to shout, to let her anger out, but the door to the room opened and the monk returned as if he knew what was about to happen. He took her back to her room. Isa ignored her as she left. Zoja's last sight of the elderly woman was the vision of her opening poisoned jars of jam and tasting each lightly with her finger as she tried to decide which one she would put on her bread. Later, as she sat in her sparse cell, a different kind of music came to her through the stone gardens. Zoja didn't know if it meant that Isa was dead, but she hoped so. She hoped the monk was discovering just how awful the divinity of the Red King was.

When she said that to us, Signe laughed. Don't you have faith? she asked from her bottom bunk. Signe had kept her faith in the Red King. She'd been homeless and living on the streets before she was sent to the red labyrinth. She had always been faithful to the Red King, but this faith only grew after she arrived, as if the red labyrinth itself offered not just support for her belief but also an explanation and a curious absolution for all that had happened and was happening to her.

'The Red King is a lie,' Zoja said to the hollow darkness of our room. 'He was born a man and remains a man even after all these centuries. The Red King was said to be a great king, but not because he was just, or fair, because he was none of those things. He was great because he was powerful. He thought of himself as someone who was more than just a king. Early on in his rule, he outlawed the use of his name because he thought it allowed people to identify with him. If people saw him as equal, he wrote, then his authority was not absolute. He demanded to be called the Red King and the Red King he has been since. Books that held his name were burnt. Those who shared it were sentenced to death. The Red King was so successful in doing this that within a generation his real name was forgotten. We don't know it, even now. This is partly because as his reign continued, so did his dreams of power. He built giant armies and conquered all the lands on this continent. He destroyed the cultures and languages that existed. He melted currencies and tore down statues and burnt art. He hired scholars to write histories that were nothing more than fiction. He had them read aloud in the streets, or performed at festivals. He allowed only those most loyal to learn how to read and write and banned it from the rest of his people. He wanted his subjects bound to him. He wanted them to be incapable of imagining a world without him.

'He rejected marriage for a long time. Because of his power, because of what he was capable of, he thought nothing of children or his legacy. He built himself a capital by the harbour and began to think about conquering the lands afar. This occupied him until, one day, he met a beautiful and powerful woman. There are many stories about her but none of them tell you her name. Some of the stories claim she was a pirate. Others say she was a soldier who had led the Red King's armies during his most recent battles. The Red King himself said she'd been made by the earth. She was a gift to him, a being unlike any other. Most scholars believe she was an offer from the kingdoms across the sea, an offer of peace. The kingdoms had been sending him precious gifts for years so that he would stay in his part of the world. No one knows why this woman was different, if she was an offering. After she married the Red King she took the name of the Black Queen. There are no paintings or sketches of her, just as there are none of the Red King. For all we know the Black Queen could have been twenty-two, thirty-eight, or twelve at the time she married the Red King. We don't know. We know that their marriage was celebrated by a grand feast that lasted for a year. The feasts were held in the centre of every city and town and village. When you ate at it, you saw visions of a sky with no stars. After the year was over, the Red King and Black Queen ruled together. They ruled for a decade before the Black Queen fell pregnant. She gave birth to twins.

'We know their names just as we know our own. Zoja. Signe. Emy. These and more were the names of the twins. They were given all of the known names, regardless of gender. The official records of their name filled countless books and those books are used now by parents to name their children. But the birth of the twins did not bring joy. Within months they were dead. It is said that their names were still being written when they died. We do not know what illness was the cause, or what other reasons might have led to the deaths. We only know that they died and that with those deaths the Red King and Black Queen were changed. They saw a world, suddenly, of chaos. They saw a world that, despite all their power and all their might, they could not fully control. They began to see themselves as vessels who knelt before some undefined rule of the universe that was neither stated or given over to comprehension. Some scholars say that the Red King was so distraught by this realisation that he considered destroying his own kingdom but was stopped by the Black Queen. Some say it was the other way round. However it went, they did not destroy their kingdom, but decided to make a new one, one that allowed them to exist beyond their new intolerable awareness of grief.

'The Red King and the Black Queen sought out witches and warlocks. They sought out anyone and everyone who had some knowledge of the unknown. They knew much themselves but still they sought more. They sought everything. With that knowledge they started to build a world that would be able to exist outside this one. The first structures that they built were not deep within the ground, but above it. It was reported that the structures were both beautiful and terrible in their form but also singular. We call it the labyrinth now because of what we see around us, but it is said that the labyrinth originally had a name that is now lost to us. It was said that the Red King and the Black Queen layered their creation with all the power they had to shift them beyond mortal design. There are some stories that say some people tried to stop them when they realised what they were doing. These people were sorcerers from the black sea, or rulers from kingdoms across the sea, people who had until now feared the Red King and the Black Queen but wouldn't stand against them. Unsurprisingly, these people failed. The Red King and the Black Queen killed those who came against them. Then they killed those who aided them in the labyrinth's creation, who helped them build their new world. The histories are all very clear on this. In doing this the Red King and the Black Queen ensured that all the knowledge that had helped build the labyrinth was kept only by themselves. They alone would remain the repositories of the designs and spells that they had used. They alone would know how to undo their awful creation.

'It is said that the labyrinth took a hundred years to be built. Scholars estimate that thousands upon thousands of people died during its creation, as nearly did the Red King and the Black Queen. But they did not die, clearly. Instead they entered the labyrinth. Once they entered it sunk into the ground. For years terrible earthquakes followed. There are reports that outside our nation there were great tidal waves and floods. The lands outside our own were shattered and new ones emerged from the ocean. People believed that it was deliberate, that those nations were punished for trying to stop the Red King and the Black Queen. Regardless if that was true or not, the opening of the labyrinth changed the world in such a dramatic way that it became a subject of such mythology that it is difficult to know what is real now and what is not. What we do know is that somewhere in those years the labyrinth was split. The Red King took his half and the Black Queen her half. We don't know why. For many years we heard nothing from them and knew nothing of this divide. Then the red and black monks emerged to tell us about it. They divided the kingdom in the name of the Red King and the Black Queen. They made councils in their names to rule. They built monasteries over the entrances to the red and black labyrinths and told us of new laws and who would enact them. They told us the Red King and Black Queen were gods now. They watched us from their own kingdoms within their labyrinths. They judged how we lived. They would reward and punish us in life and death, they said. At first, only the worst of us, only the most truly heinous, were sent to the labyrinths alive. But we know all that did not last. All of us who sit here right now, all of us who live in the Red King's labyrinth, know that we have not been sent here because of our crimes, just as no one in the Black Queen's labyrinth was sent because of theirs. And we know the Red King and the Black Queen are not gods, either, because we are here in their new world. We know that for all their power, they simply made a prison for the living and the dead, where one is forced to serve the other for all eternity.'

7

AFTER that night Zoja started to tell us regularly about what she had read. She spoke mostly about history, about the history the Red King, the Black Queen and their monks worked to keep hidden. She told us about failed revolutions, secret executions, and diplomatic protests from other nations, as well as sanctions and blockades that we knew nothing about. She recited the lost names of the nations the Red King and Black Queen had destroyed. She drew a map to show us where they'd once been. At first, she told all of this to Emy, Signe and me. Then she told it to others in the dormitory. As more and more people asked her questions, she started to hold court in our cramped dining rooms. Some were reluctant to attend at first, but that changed after a while. We'd already paid the price, after all. So had Zoja. Before she came to the red labyrinth, Zoja had been careful. She told us how she had kept what she knew secret. She hid the fact that she could read. She never taught people how to read or read to people. But here she was, a prisoner within the earth anyway. Why shouldn't she tell us now? Why shouldn't we listen? Why shouldn't she teach? Why shouldn't we learn? Even those who held faith with the Red King like Signe agreed. It was Signe, in fact, who suggested we use the bones of butchered animals to write on. We would leave this behind later, when we got access to the gardens and could use what was there, could grow secret crops to make papyrus, but at first we wrote on bones. They were broken, smashed into shards so that they were easy to smuggle in our robes from the restaurant to the dormitory. We made ink during our shifts as well. We took precautions but it wasn't hard to hide from the monks. The monks brought us food and clothing and made sure we were assigned jobs. They watched us and didn't like idle hands but they had grown lazy over the years and were more interested in their own lives and their own internal politics. They searched for knives under our beds and in dressers and then went their way, back to their lives of luxury.

None of us thought we were part of an insurrection, or whatever else you've heard what we did called. A revolution? A rebellion? I've heard it said, just as you have. But none of us thought we would ever leave the red labyrinth. Zoja especially. As far as she was concerned, she was going to spend the rest of her life here. She spent some time trying to make a map of what was around us, like we all do at one point, but she was no more successful than I was. The red labyrinth resisted us. After Zoja gave up trying to map the paths around us, she spent her time trying to recreate the texts she had read. She was mostly successful, but there was no one else who had read the stories she had, no one who even knew of them, and thus no one to double check her work. Zoja was frustrated by this. Once I heard her and Lo fall into an argument about how she was doing everything and Lo was doing nothing. It wasn't true. Lo was teaching us the language of the labyrinths, doing it behind the monks' backs. She was taking quite the risk, but she didn't know the histories any more than I did. I told Zoja this. She got angry with me and left our room for a while. Later we found out she was living with a man. She apologised after she moved back in with us, somewhat sheepishly. She had a few relationships in the dormitory. I tell you that so you know she was just a regular woman trying to live what life she had. The three of us didn't like any of the men Zoja lived with. Zoja was a little like the adult daughter none of us had ever raised and we were protective of her. Truthfully, we wouldn't have let her start a revolution. If Zoja had said to us that she was thinking of raising an army, of attacking the monks and taking the red labyrinth, all three of us would have sat her down and talked her out of it. But it was never said. I know how it sounds. I know how it looks, even. I have a sword, after all.

But nothing was planned. Nothing was imagined. We learned about histories we didn't know. Zoja taught us about medicines we could use. We adapted it the best we could to what was in the red labyrinth. We had lessons on how to read and write. We used the smuggled shards of bone to write on. We helped teach the others, like Zoja did after she learned the language of the labyrinths. A few years later I began to teach people how to read. I recited the histories I had heard. This is how we lived until Zoja disappeared.

It happened on the day a monk came again to the dormitory and asked for Zoja. The monk was a grey haired, matronly woman. She wore a red robe that showed none of her tattoos. She was quiet and gave the impression that she held a minor position. We worried that she'd come to move Zoja to a different area, to somewhere else within the red labyrinth. It wasn't unheard of. When Zoja didn't come back, that's what we thought happened. Some of us said Zoja had been moved to a new kitchen, or to a stand. Zoja had regained her strength by then and she was able to pull a cart and stand on a street for a day. Some others said she'd gone somewhere else like the gardens. We all had a theory, or a fear. I had mine, as well, but I was wrong, just like the others. None of us thought that Zoja had been taken to the Red King's throne, to the building that shifted and moved as if it had been made and remade a thousand times over a thousand years and was now stuck in a loop, searching for its final form.

The inside of the building was free of this chaos, however. Zoja described it to us later as eerily still and silent. The monk who'd come through the door with her was gone. She stood alone in a large room, a hall really, not so dissimilar to one an old king would have sat in back in the days when a kingdom numbered fifty or so thatched roofs and burned easily. Zoja found herself walking through it even though she couldn't remember starting to walk. The floors were made from polished stone and looked to be full of crushed stars, stars from a sky she didn't recognise. Occasionally she thought she saw something in the debris, a face, maybe, or a body. It was hard to be sure. She couldn't stop walking though she wanted to. She wanted to look at what she was walking over. It was like being in a dream. She had a vague sense of vertigo. She forced herself to look away from the floor, from the images she was starting to think looked like worlds, new worlds imagined by someone other than herself. Ahead of her was a light. It was a curious light because it was the only one in the hall. The light grew as Zoja drew closer. Soon, she realised that it wasn't contained behind glass, but was free, as if it was in a pit or even out in the open, except this wasn't true.

The fire was a man. It was, she saw as she came closer, a man who was on fire. He was sitting on a stone throne, quite alive, and watching her while he burned without warmth, while his skin was turned dark and devoured and he showed no pain. He was a tall man, full of long, thin limbs and a narrow, sharp face. The flames had replaced his hair, and they flickered and flashed there, tasting the oxygen that surrounded his thin gold crown. He wore a robe of ash. It was very fine and it looked like it would crumble from his body at any moment.

Zoja Rose, said the man on fire in a dry rasp. His lips did not move. *Do I need to introduce myself?*

'No,' she said, because he did not.

Some would ask for forgiveness at the sight of me, the Red King said. *Some for mercy. But you ask for neither, I see.*

She tried to reply, but found that the compelling sense of movement that had brought her now compelled her to remain silent.

You have nothing to say to me that I will find interesting. Instead, I will talk to you and you will listen. I may not be a god, like you have said, but I am more than you. I will always be more than you. You should remember that.

The Red King touched Zoja's face even though he did not move. She could feel his hand, his burning hand, running along her chin. She could not describe the sensation easily because it felt like nothing tangible. Instead, she found herself lost in thoughts and visions, none of them hers. They rushed through her, overwhelming herself, flooded her with memories and images. She saw the dead in the red labyrinth. She saw them unlike she'd seen them before, with an anguish she couldn't turn from. She saw a beautiful woman holding a warped crown of wasps. She saw a child wrapped in white. She saw a blurred book. Then, as abruptly as it started, it ended. Zoja found herself looking at a still, burning face.

You and I share captivity, the Red King said. *My monks have judged you to be sinful and have brought you here to my prison of sins. We are slaves to my labyrinth and to them. Once they begged to be made immortal and I said I would make them so but first they must live and die. I should never have allowed them to live. The mis-*

take was mine. In life they are all different and in that difference they have forgotten my rule and my power. They make their own laws now. They think they honour my legacy when they do this but they do not. I do not want my world to be a prison. I do not want to be a prisoner in it.

Zoja heard her skin crack apart. The fire from the Red King was breaking her open. She had never before felt such pain. The flames slipped through her skin, through her muscles, her teeth, and her bones. Her body offered no resistance to what was quickly becoming an act of consumption. She lost all sense of herself. She was no longer whole, but was made from millions and millions of particles, all of which were being broken again and again.

I see everything in my labyrinth, the Red King said. His voice was around her. She no longer had any vision, could not see the Red King or his throne or hall. *I know everything that happens,* he continued. *It was meant to be a place for eternal life but it is broken and I wish to be free of it. You will help me be free of it, young Zoja Rose.*

Suddenly the Red King's face was before her. It was free of flames, the skin withered and burnt. It was so desiccated that it pressed against his skull as if it were a tattoo on his bones, an intricate design that had been done after his flesh had been stripped away. His eyes were worse. They were ruined sockets full of ash, filled with burning embers. It was the embers that saw her.

My proposition is simple. The Red King's cracked lips moved but the voice Zoja heard came from somewhere else. *Not so long ago, my queen escaped her labyrinth. A monk helped her. His name was Eero. He remade the lost texts that my queen and I used to build the labyrinth. The dead helped him. My queen and I made a place to teach Eero and another to break the labyrinth. We could not do it ourselves. We are chained to this labyrinth and we cannot break our own chains. It is part of our failure that this is so. That is why Eero exists. He was taught how to recreate the spells that made the labyrinth. He was to free my queen. Another was to free me, but when she died, Eero was to do it. But instead, he fled my queen's service. My monks searched for him. They did this on my order and on their own and they refused to bring him to me when they found him. They took him back to my queen's labyrinth. I have no power there. They know I don't and they hold him there now. They have told me this. They ignore me when I order them to bring Eero to me. They treat me now like I am one of you, one of their prisoners. So I must turn to your kind for help. I must turn to those who share my captivity. But I must turn to someone more, as well. I must turn to someone who can learn by herself, someone who can do what Eero did with or without his help.* The Red King paused. It was a long pause. *You know Eero,* he said, finally. *That will help as well.*

Zoja found herself, suddenly, lying on the floor. She was shivering. The tiles were dark now. There was no cracked stardust within them, no sense of another world, or a vision of existence that she couldn't comprehend. The throne was gone, the Red King as well. As Zoja lay there, her pain became dull and localised. It ran along the right side of her body, divided on an invisible line that bisected her. Zoja stood weakly and pushed back the sleeve of her right arm. There, along her skin, were fresh tattoos. They were red labyrinth tattoos, so violent in colour that Zoja worried her skin had been split open. It wasn't, but the tattoos ran over hand, over the stump of her missing finger, then up her arm, and over her chest and pelvis and leg, much as Ozias' tattoos had.

My monks will hunt you. The Red King's voice was a fading whisper in her ear, but she didn't know which ear. *The one who brought you to me is loyal, but others are not. They will know about you soon enough. They will know what I have done. They will kill you if they catch you.*

8

ZOJA suddenly heard footsteps. She couldn't focus on where they were coming from because nothing sounded right in the absence of the Red King's voice. For a moment, she thought the steps were in her head, that within her was a staircase and a room that she'd been locked in, like a miniature orphan. She started to limp down the hall to escape her thoughts and the steps she heard. The limp was temporary, a stiffness from what the Red King had done to her, and it faded as she walked. She was glad. She was worried about what he had done to her. She didn't know all of its implications, but she knew some. She knew she couldn't return to the dormitory. No one there had tattoos like the ones she now had. It would be impossible to hide them. The robes the monks provided did not cover her hands, or enough of her neck. There was a single line that reached up behind her ear, that was the length of her missing finger, and which drew the eye immediately. Worse, if the monks found her in the dormitory, they would punish the rest as well. Zoja wanted to curse the Red King. If he had wanted her to escape the red labyrinth he could have given her a map she could hold and could look at, rather than scarring her body. He could have shown her to the door as well, Zoja thought sourly as she continued to walk through the echoing throne room. She'd never leave the red labyrinth if she could not leave the throne room. Maybe that was the point? The Red King was cruel. He could leave her trapped until she died. As if in response to her thought, a hallway appeared.

Zoja stepped into it. The sound of footsteps faded. The light did as well. Soon Zoja was in darkness. It engulfed her, consumed her, then released her. When it did, she found herself standing on a small pathway within the red labyrinth. It was a dead-end path, hidden between a series of roads and bridges that over and underlapped it. It was one of those small ends that were peppered throughout the red labyrinth, that seemed to exist for the sole purpose of frustrating those who wanted to map the world they were trapped in. This dead end, Zoja could see, was far into the red labyrinth, so far in fact that she could no longer see the continuously shifting building that was the Red King's throne room. Yet, it was from that building she had emerged. She couldn't imagine its interior stretched out to where she was standing, to the dark where she was, but she knew that it did by virtue that she was there no matter how incomprehensible it was. But then, didn't that describe the red labyrinth itself? There was no logical sense to it. No reason. She wasn't surprised when she realised that there was no door for her to step back into, no way for her to retrace her steps and return to the Red King and his throne.

Zoja had no idea where she was. She looked over the ledge and saw blooms of light falling through the smoky air, lighting up buildings and lanes like lost nightmares from dreamers in another world. She recognised nothing. There was a large open rock garden full of succulents and tall, strangely shaped white plants. There were dormitories, but unlike the one she'd lived in, these looked newer, the cut rock that had been used to make them not yet stained by the everlasting smoke of the red labyrinth. The dead were different as well. This was a surprise to Zoja because she thought the dead couldn't change, that they were complete as pale, washed out memories of themselves. But the dead she saw now had more colour. They had traces of red in them. Their faces contained the looks of anguish she had seen while with the Red King. But worse, Zoja thought, was that it looked like the dead were aware of the half-lives they were trapped in and the actions they were taking. They could very well be the dreamers of this awful world, powerless to stop themselves from doing what they were.

Zoja couldn't stay where she was. Some monks would pass soon and notice her, or a prisoner would see her and report her. The latter needn't be a malicious act. Prisoners got lost in the red labyrinth and Zoja was certainly lost. Another prisoner might spot her from a distance and believe she'd been abandoned by monks for amusement, or had taken a chance to escape and walked as far as she could before her food and water ran out. Of course, there were also prisoners who'd report her to earn favour with the monks. Zoja knew that as well. Everyone had their own acts of survival in the red labyrinth. I know there are things that I did that I'm not proud of. I'll admit that as we sit here, as I talk to you and the cold starts to pick up. I did things I wasn't proud of in the red labyrinth. I did them for reasons that shame me now.

Zoja never did. She never compromised. She wouldn't now, either. She climbed a small staircase that was near her, turned left down a road, then right into an alleyway. At the end of it she could see the edge of the red labyrinth, the rugged open earth, massive and oppressive. She could see, also, the digging crews stretched across it, attached to the soil in a network of harnesses and platforms. This was how the red labyrinth grew, she knew, but she was still stunned to see it. She'd never been close to the edges before. Since her arrival, Zoja had lived without the sense of how big the red labyrinth actually was. It didn't end there, she knew, as there were tunnels that led deep into the earth and connected the red labyrinth to the black. At least, that was what she'd heard over the years of her captivity, and what she'd read. But to be faced with it… Zoja found herself strangely stilled by it despite the danger she was in.

She was standing in an alley next to a school. On the other side of the new wall was a large playground marked with chalk for various games and beyond that a series of classrooms and dorms that held not just students, but monks as well. There were dozens of monks who lived on the school grounds, whose task was to not just teach the children their ways and languages, but to watch over them as well. The monks were very protective of their children. They lived in fear that if the prisoners rose up, the first place they would strike would be the schools throughout the red labyrinth. The fear, I can tell you, wasn't unjustified. When I had been in the brothel I had heard many women talk about escaping and finding their children as they did. I was one of them, in fact. I would dream of the children I'd never seen. It was always difficult because of the memory of the violence that had born them, but still I dreamed of my lost children and when awake, a part of me wanted to act on my dreams. For their part, the monks knew this. There were never more protected places than the schools. There were always guards and always patrols.

Zoja was grabbed from behind. She was caught so suddenly that she couldn't fight back effectively, couldn't twist, or kick, or even scream. A rough, gloved hand was over her mouth. It had a foul smell and she gagged repeatedly while trying to take a breath. Roughly, she was thrown into the back of a cart, pushed up against equally foul-smelling barrels that sloshed disgustingly as she hit them. 'Don't make a sound,' a voice hissed. It was a man's voice, a voice she recognised but couldn't place. The man, she saw from within the cart, wore a robe like herself, but with the hood pulled down so Zoja couldn't make out his face. 'You make a sound and they'll kill us both,' he said and grabbed the covering on the cart, pulling it down. It locked Zoja in a fetid, awful air. It was only then that she realised that what she was next to was full waste barrels. She placed her hand over mouth to stop herself from gagging.

She heard another man's voice outside the cart. 'You going to get us killed, Jacek. They fucking saw her.'

'They just saw some robes,' Jacek said. 'Now shut up, the monks are coming.'

Zoja heard the monks. One of them spoke to Jacek and the other man in a language they could understand, while the second talked in the language of the labyrinths. The second monk wasn't saying anything insightful. He was mostly complaining about the smell of the cart, and about the smell of the two men pulling it. The first monk agreed, because after a few questions, the monks left and the cart started to roll, pulled by the two men out of the alley and onto the road.

Zoja tried not to make any noise, but it was difficult. Every jostle of the cart, every crack in the road, every bump the wheels hit made her feel as if she was going to be sick. She gagged repeatedly. When Jacek pulled back the covering she did in fact throw up, turning over the edge of the cart and vomiting on the dirty ground. The man with Jacek laughed. He was a big, dirty man wearing dirty robes. On the streets of the red labyrinth he would have stood out, but inside the waste depot, everyone and everything was dirty.

Zoja sat on a small step of stairs while Jacek and the other man emptied the cart. She'd never been to a waste depot before, or even near one. She was familiar with the carts, though. Everyone was. They were pulled by two prisoners along a set route through the red labyrinth each day, collecting barrels of shit and piss and more. Waste collectors had some of the longest tattoos on their bodies because their routes often stretched over multiple levels. They were also, Zoja knew, some of the most shunned prisoners. The smells they lived in seeped into their clothes, their hair, and their skin. Even the monks kept their distance, paying only cursory visits to their dormitories when they must, when new prisoners arrived or there were disturbances.

Jacek had grown a beard since Zoja had last seen him. It wasn't well kept, but then nothing about him was. He was tall and thin still, but there was a ragged roughness about him that she hadn't previously seen. After he finished unloading the cart he came to her and took her by the arm wordlessly. There were stairs at the back and he led her up, up multiple floors until he came to the final one. He didn't talk to her at any point and she thought about stopping him and asking what was going on. She wasn't convinced he meant her no harm, but then he stopped in front of a door. It was an actual door, painted red.

He knocked. The man who answered it was small and thin and wore an eye patch. His hands were stained with ash, but he was otherwise neat and clean. There was something familiar about him, but Zoja couldn't place it until the man said her name in quiet shock. 'Nathaniel?' she said in response, hardly believing her eyes.

'I found her out on the streets,' Jacek said once they were in the room, inside what was a large office. The window in it looked over a smoky street, but the office itself was filled with designs drawn in ash and drawn on the walls. They looked a lot like labyrinth tattoos. 'She was just standing next to the school, can you believe that? I didn't realise who she was at first. I just saw her from behind. I grabbed her, and that's when I saw who it was, and I saw her tattoos. Well, some of them. They're all over her body.'

'Are they?' Nathaniel asked. 'Are they truly all over you?'

Just the right side, she explained. She told them both what had happened. She told them, in part, because she needed to hear it herself, to ground it in a reality that might not make sense of it, but would at least assure her it was real.

'Do you believe what the Red King said?' Nathaniel asked after she finished. 'Do you trust him?'

'He's cruel and mad,' she said. 'I don't know if he was those things before he made the labyrinth, but he is them now. He wants nothing more than to leave. He believes that he is being kept here against his will. The monks are his enemy now. That's why he sent me here, why he put me where you are. You and your maps.'

'You mean he knows about this?' Nathaniel waved at the walls, at the illustrations on it. 'This is just our routes. I'm charged with making sure our routes are run, and this—'

Jacek laughed bitterly. 'The Red King knows,' he said. 'He's just like the Black Queen. He knows everything that is happening around him. He's a god, remember?' Jacek turned to Zoja. 'I saw the Black Queen while I was a soldier, remember. I told you about her when we were in that jail, but I was afraid to say her name. I thought she might hear me. At night, I dreamed about her. I still dream about her, still dream that she is walking across the burning fields, destroying everything in her path to remake it anew. She always knew where we were. Where the soldiers were, I mean. It was why we were losing so poorly. It's why we were being decimated out there. That's the news you never heard.'

'Then the Red King knows,' the other man said and shrugged. 'It is what it is. We cannot change what we have done, or what we plan to do.'

Zoja knew what they planned to do. They were planning to escape the red labyrinth. They were mapping it in their carts, recording it here in this office with the burnt ends of sticks. They had not gotten far, she could tell, but they had gotten further than anyone else she had known. She could help them, though. They, in turn, could help her. She couldn't read her body without help. Maybe that was why the Red King sent her there. Maybe it was not. He certainly didn't send her out of kindness, Zoja knew. But he might've sent her out of necessity and desperation. Imagine, she said to the two men. Imagine if the red labyrinth was truly mapped, and everyone knew the routes throughout? Imagine if they could find the stairs that led out. There's more than one exit. We know that. 'The exits will be fortified,' Zoja said. 'But if we're organised, if everyone is organised, we might be able to leave.'

'You want to do this?' Nathaniel said. 'You want to betray the Red King and rise up against him?'

'I will go to the black labyrinth like I said I would. I will find Eero. I will learn all that I can and honour our agreement.'

'You cannot free him!' Jacek was horrified. 'Have you no sense of mercy for those who still live above us?'

'No,' Zoja said. 'And if the Red King is listening, he should know that this is my price for helping him.'

9

ZOJA spent the next week hiding in the waste depot, spent the week living in Nathaniel's office while he copied out the tattoos on her body. In the end, the copy he made covered not just the walls, but the ceiling and the floor. It was so extensive that it reached out the door and into the hallway, ashy and delicate and otherworldly. Later, I asked Zoja if she felt threatened while she stood there naked before Nathaniel, letting him copy all the places the lines went across her. At first, she said. But only at first. Within a day, she realised she was the one who had the power, not Nathaniel or Jacek or any of the other prisoners who lived and worked in the depot. Part of this power came from her tattoos. They weren't like the ones the others had. They had not been made with ink. No one could describe what they'd been made with, but they all agreed that no ink looked like that on skin, or felt like that to the touch. Zoja tried to remember if Ozias' tattoos had felt different to her but the memories were too faint, too far away. But it wasn't just the tattoos that gave her power over the others. It was the fragility of those around her, the desperation they lived in, and the need that had buried inside them, the wish for someone, or something, to offer hope. Zoja's presence was a response to that and the other prisoners viewed her not as one of them, or as a person, or a woman, but as a sacred figure. Because of that, Nathaniel's touch was never inappropriate. His tone was always respectful. A prisoner brought her meals, was happy to serve her. Others stepped out of her way, gave her space. When Zoja left the depot, all the prisoners gathered to see her leave. They gave her a pack with a map of the red labyrinth sewn into it, a well-made knife, and a promise that they would organise the other prisoners in the red labyrinth.

It would take years for them to do this. I lived through it. I know. I could spend weeks telling you about how it happened, about the people who were instrumental, about the networks that were created, about the major triumphs and setbacks. I could tell you how the first maps we circulated were treated with distrust and how prisoners thought they were traps. I could tell you how the maps were never quite right, how streets went in the opposite direction, or buildings in the wrong place, no matter how much we updated or fixed them. I could tell you how communication in the red labyrinth was difficult and how hard trust was to win. It was especially hard when the Red King's loyal monks joined us. They appeared three months after Zoja disappeared into the tunnels, after she entered the darkness that bridged the red labyrinth to the black. The monks who came to us were led by the middle-aged woman who'd come for Zoja on the Red King's command. Her name was Tamasa. She told us that Zoja had reached the black labyrinth and that she was here at the Red King's command. Tamasa was a hard woman. Unlike many of the loyalists, she knew the Red King was mad. She once told me that the Red King was incapable of honouring any agreement struck between him and Zoja. I would be a fool to believe he'd respect my freedom after he'd won his own, she said. Tamasa was the person who made me question my faith in Zoja and what she was doing. She was going to free the Red King. She was going to free a mad god. It didn't matter that the Red King wasn't a god, because he wasn't a man either. He had lived thousands of years. He had power that was unrivalled. The only thing that kept him in check was the red labyrinth. Surely my own incarceration was a price I would be willing to pay to continue that? Surely Zoja thought the same. But she had struck a deal. Tamasa was clear on that. Zoja had named her price and the price was our freedom. There were days when my doubts about what we were doing almost crippled me. It didn't help that we were allied beside the Red King's loyal monks. Tamasa saved my life one day. She killed a monk who was strangling me with her bare hands. We became friends. Worse, lovers. How could I justify it? How could Zoja? Jacek would tell us stories of the Black Queen wandering above us, wearing her twisted crown of wasps and laying waste to everything that opposed her. I could do nothing but question my loyalty. The others did the same. Emy murdered Lo and Signe murdered Emy in response. We held to our belief like Tamasa to her own in the Red King. I could find no easy answers. No one could, not even Zoja.

She was on her own journey and it was difficult. Her passage between the labyrinths was hard. We believe it took her three months because that is what the Red King said it took. Zoja herself doesn't know. They were days in the dark, she told me later. Days of suffering. Days where you wished you were dead.

Zoja's food ran out early in the tunnels. Her water soon after. She'd taken what she could from the prisoners, but it wasn't enough. She had hoped that crossing between the two labyrinths would be easy, and that she would do it within the limit of her supplies, but some of the tunnels had collapsed and the paths she thought she knew no longer existed. She had light, but used it sparingly. She navigated mostly in the dark by feel. The map sewn into her bag became suggestive, the memory of a lover's body from years past. She thought of Ozias often. The Red King had called him Eero. It was the name Jan had asked her for but now that she knew it, it was nothing to her. Ozias might as well be Eero for all he meant to her after four years in the red labyrinth. Zoja had left the life he had been part of behind. She'd had no choice. Ozias was a fleeting, momentary fantasy. She wanted to think of him as dead. She would be dead soon, she believed. She was starving. She was dying of thirst. If she was out of the Red King's reach, maybe she was in Ozias'. He wasn't a god. There were no gods. But Zoja needed comfort and the memory of an old lover was her only comfort. Yet she didn't die. For some reason days passed without food and water and she did not collapse, or descend into delirium. She exhausted her light in a dead end, completely lost. She couldn't bear it anymore. She sat and cried out of hunger and thirst and desperation until she fell asleep.

When she woke up, the passage was flooded in red light. The light came from her tattoos. It was, at first, blinding. She worried that something terrible had happened to her. Later, she realised that it already had. The Red King had changed her more than she'd realised. The tattoos were more than just a map, they were the physical representation of his power, a power he'd used to warp and twist her body into something he desired her to be. Zoja wasn't dying, but she still felt hunger and thirst. She couldn't escape the desperate need within her. She had to learn to suppress it, to control it. She had more luck controlling the light that came from her tattoos. Soon enough, she could get her hand to light up alone. She used it like a torch while she searched for a path to take her across to the black labyrinth. She could flash the light in the palm of her hand and make her tattoos light up and follow a path of her choosing across her skin. She could not use it to clear the debris she encountered regularly.

You could argue that Zoja should have been grateful for what the Red King had done to her. Some people do. But she wasn't. She had not asked for it. She had not consented to it. She did not know the extent of his changes, or the limits, and this bothered her. She thought of Jan. The servant mirrored the master.

Zoja tried to rearrange her tattoos, but couldn't. She stopped going to the bathroom. The pain she felt from hunger lingered. How was she chained to the Red King? she asked. The last question was the most important. Zoja worried that it meant she would never be fully in control of herself, that the Red King would be able to usurp control over her whenever he wished. His authority over her would be total if this was true. She would become her own labyrinth, both prisoner and jailer. Who knew what he would do when she was done with his task.

Eventually, Zoja found the entrance to the black labyrinth. A passage led to another passage, one where the floor had given way. Down that break, beyond two twists and half a collapsed wall, was a door made from stone. It was a thick door with red and black hand prints overlapping it. It was so thick that Zoja would never have been able to open herself. Fortunately, it was split down the middle. Beyond it lay another set of tunnels much like the ones she had been in for months now. The only difference was that rather than a barely usable map, she now had none. The map on her ended at this point, crossed over to the left side of her body, to where Ozias' tattoos had been. Zoja would have to find her own way through the broken tunnels, make her own path through the ruins, until she reached the black labyrinth itself.

It didn't take her nearly as long as it did in the red labyrinth. This was mostly due to the damage the tunnels had suffered. Many had collapsed and become nothing more than earth, but in doing so, had created a new tunnel. It was more, actually, of an opening than a tunnel. It was a jagged wound that cut through the extremely unstable earth. More than once, Zoja lost her footing as the ground began to collapse. She saw the earth open and close before her and behind her. She saw it ripple both above and below as if it were alive. Every step she took was terrifying. Any moment, she believed, she would be buried alive. She was afraid to move. She was more afraid to stop. She only did when she was completely exhausted. She shone as much red light out of herself as she could, looking for the end.

Then, suddenly, the black labyrinth was before her. The earth fell away, turned into a ragged cliff that revealed a huge darkness that was broken apart with luminescent light. The light came from glowworms and, though the worms never came to the structure of the black labyrinth itself, they collected at the edges and borders of the earth. Their light revealed the remains of the black labyrinth, shining on its fallen paths, its twisted roads, and its crumbling buildings like a broken skyline. The darkness that remained gave the impression that it was on the edge of overcoming the light. It overcame Zoja's, certainly. Her light got lost in the darkness while she walked through the black labyrinth's ruin.

In terms of size, the black labyrinth was similar to the red. It was impossible to comprehend its full size by simple gaze and Zoja's mind struggled to fully appreciate its immensity. In an attempt to navigate it, Zoja briefly entertained the idea that both the red and black labyrinths were twins and that her map would be good for the other. This proved to be a mistake. Zoja learned that quickly enough, learned it while searching for food and water, learned it almost to the point of disaster. She was forced to wander the massive, broken world without a guide. There were many times when her path was impossible. There were times when she found herself walking in circles, or at dead ends. She wished she had a direction she had to go in. It would have made it easier. As it was, Zoja wandered without direction. She was looking for Ozias. She was looking for Jan. She was looking for Jan's silent monks. They were somewhere within these ruins, but were they up, or down, or behind her or in front of her? It was an impossible task to make that decision uninformed. The dark became oppressive the longer she walked through it, the longer she went without finding anyone. She spent years wandering the black labyrinth, trapped in a solitude that few can imagine.

Then one day, one day as Zoja made her way to a shallow rock pool lit by luminescent glowworms, she came across a camp.

10

SHE would not have recognised Jan if not for his knives and jars that were set on one side of the camp, similar to his room in the monastery. He wasn't well. He was sickly thin, coughing continuously, and reliant on a cane. The cane was poorly made and splintered at the bottom. Still, he used it to push himself up from his messy bed, a bed full of dirty blankets and scattered books. His fingers were stained with ink. He'd grown a scraggly, grey beard that did not hide the red tattoo on his neck, the tattoo that wound around the right of his thin throat like a broken noose. 'Zoja,' he said in a scratchy voice. 'You're not who I thought I would see. I have prayed to the Red King in my need. I hoped he would return my children to me so that they could finish my work.'

'Did the Red King take them?'

'The labyrinth took them. The black labyrinth, I mean. It poisons us every moment we are here. You must be careful—'

Zoja stepped back, stepped away from his touch. 'So you're still loyal to the Red King, then?'

'Should I not be?' Jan left the space between them. He leaned on his cane heavily and looked around his camp, at the disarray he lived in. 'Well, perhaps you might worry that I have lost my way. I can see that. Certainly my peers have lost their way. They question our god. They question his plans. I had hoped they'd learned the error of their ways, but it seems things have gotten worse. I never imagined that the Red King would be forced to rely upon one like you.'

'A prisoner, you mean?'

'A prisoner who knew Eero.' He waved his free hand at the bed, at the books on and around it. 'I know why he has sent you,' he said. 'I know why he is impatient. I promise you I have got as much as I can out of him. I've used all my skill and all I have is fragments. Eero has been difficult. He is still difficult. I suppose I shouldn't be surprised. He was blessed by the Black Queen, after all. He still has that blessing even though he has rejected her. He believes the Black Queen sacrificed all the families that were kept here and all the history she had saved for her freedom. He does not believe she had the right to do that.'

Zoja didn't respond. She didn't trust Jan. She doubted that he was a loyal monk of the Red King. She'd listened to him talk like this while she'd been his prisoner. One of his great strengths as a torturer was that he had been able to create the illusion that the pair of them were equal, that they shared a prison despite their positions, and because of that, he could confide as freely in her as she could in him. He created a false commonality between the two of them. He did it so well that, in the depths of her captivity, Zoja had believed him when he said that they were both victims of the situation they were in. They had both been stripped of their power. They were both subjects of a force far greater than either of them. It had taken Zoja years to realise the full extent of that manipulation and the insidious nature of what he said. It was not something she would forget again, now that she stood in his presence again.

Outside the camp a narrow, luminescent lit path of stone led down to a shallow pool of water. Jan took Zoja to it, talking as he did, talking in a voice that might fail him at any moment. He told her how he made ink from the glowworms. You could eat them too, he said, as they came to the water. In the middle of it was a cage made from black iron. The water covered the floor of the cage and came up to the shins of the man who was kept there, who was shackled to the bars above him. Zoja recognised Ozias immediately. Unlike Jan, he hadn't changed since she'd last seen him. His hair was longer, it was true, and his beard wilder, but he had not been ill like the other man had.

'He looks like he's sleeping, but he's not,' Jan said. 'Truth be told, he doesn't sleep much, or eat or drink either. It is the Black Queen's blessing that keeps him safe from such mortal concerns. You can still hurt him, if you wish. Do you see the scars on his chest and down his legs? They are my work. I have had to do many of the base and brutal things that I don't usually do during my interrogations to Eero. He's come close to dying a few times. I admit, I've thought about killing him. There's a sickness in this black labyrinth, a curse even. It killed my children. It's killing me.' He shook his head, as if the thought had come unbidden, that it was a confession he'd not wished to make to her. 'You can talk to him if you want.'

Zoja did not, not then. Instead, she returned to the camp with Jan. He continued to talk while they walked along the passage. He told her about how he'd journeyed down flights of broken stairs and through broken doors. He described black tunnels he had to walk through. She knew what he was doing. She could feel him searching for a common experience between them, something that would allow her to let her guard down, would let her think of him as a prisoner as she was. After a while he began to talk about Ozias, though he never once called him that. He was Eero. He was never anyone but Eero. 'We thought this would be the best place to keep him,' Jan said. 'Those above me made the decision, but I agreed with it. It was here in these remains that the information to free the Red King would be found. It wasn't until later that I realised he was out of my god's reach here, as was I.' But navigating the black labyrinth out, navigating the debris with Eero after his children ailed, was more than Jan could do alone. He couldn't take him back to the Red King. He could only learn and hope that in his education he found a salvation for himself. He wrote and wrote, crushing glowworms for ink, but while he learned some of the spells needed to unbind his god, he never learned enough.

'Eero is ashamed of what he did,' Jan said. He was sitting next to a small fire, cooking a meal out of glowworms, roots, and spices. 'He says that didn't know what the Black Queen truly wanted when he freed her. He knew she wanted to return to the surface and rebuild all the world again in her vision, but he didn't realise just how violent she would be. He didn't realise she was mad. I suppose we bear some of the blame, both the red and the black monks. The orders don't talk about how our gods have been changed by the labyrinths. We don't talk about the failure of their creation. It was never meant to be a prison, you see. It was designed to be a new world for themselves and their children. It is said that there is a part of the labyrinth that we have never seen, a third part, that is lost between worlds, and that the new world is there. The monks call it the white labyrinth sometimes. The dead were meant to go there, to serve the Red King and Black Queen's children in the paradise that they'd created, but something went wrong at the time it was opened. I don't know what that was. I only know that something did go wrong. The dead were caught within the parts of the labyrinth that we see now, trapped in vast cities that were not allowed to rise above the earth as first planned. Our gods were forced to make a paradise for the dead while they themselves were trapped here.'

Except there were no dead in the black labyrinth, Zoja said. 'I've not seen a spirit since I first stepped in here.'

'You see little flickers of light occasionally, don't you?' Jan said. 'Sometimes they get lost in the luminescence around us, but they're there, like tricks of light in your eyes. Those are the dead now. They're being drawn into the black labyrinth. It still has power to draw the Black Queen's people here, but it cannot keep them. Its gift is being squandered right before our eyes.'

'Squandered?' Zoja repeated. 'I thought you agreed that the Black Queen should be free? She and the Red King?'

'They have a responsibility.' He muttered the words to himself absently and shook his head when she asked him to repeat himself. 'Never mind. It doesn't matter. How was your meal?'

She showed him the empty plate. 'Awful. The taste of those worms cannot be disguised, no matter what you cook them with.'

'Their blood is poison. Your body is warning you about it.'

'I know. When I first got here, I was so desperate to eat, that I scraped some off the side of the black labyrinth. I ate them while they were still alive. I was sick for days after. I thought I was going to die.'

'But you didn't.'

Zoja shook her head.

Jan laughed a small dry laugh.

'Maybe if I didn't know you, I would have believed you,' she said. 'But I know you don't want to free the Red King. You've no loyalty to a mad king.'

'Why do you?'

'We made a deal.'

'There are no deals you can make with the mad.' He let his plate slip from his fingers, let it fall upside down on the ground next to his cane. 'At least I will not be here to see this. I was dying before you came here. My soul was already lost. But when I saw you I knew the Red King had chosen wisely. You will learn it all. You are smart enough to do it without Eero. I knew I had to kill you, to stop you freeing him, but I also knew that I couldn't take a knife to you. You wouldn't let me get close. If I was not so weak, I could perhaps have overpowered you, but not now. Now it had to be this. Now I had to gamble with my last few weeks.' Jan's voice became slurred and desperate. 'You cannot free the Red King, Zoja! You cannot. You cannot let him and the Black Queen remake the world for their children yet again. He must stay in his prison. He must continue to serve us. He must do his duty.' He repeated his words again, his words about prisons and duty, repeated them faintly before he sank to the ground.

Jan took a while to die. Zoja sat by the fire and watched him the entire time. She thought about the time she'd cut her finger off. She rubbed at her tattooed hand, rubbed at the stump at the end of her right hand, at the phantom pain she'd not felt for years. Her finger was probably here, in one of the jars he kept full of eyes and tongues and other offerings. She would have liked to have taken her knife and stabbed him. She'd been barely able to control her fear when she first saw him, and that fear was now a rage. She listened to Jan, to his whimpers of pain and his shallow breathing coming and going like a tune she would never forget. It wasn't enough for him to die like this. Zoja's anger was bottomless. She wanted to kill him and bring him back to life and kill him again. She wanted to do it for years until her anger was sated.

There was a flicker of light through Jan's body when he died, as if something in the black labyrinth had tried to take hold of him. Zoja had seen the lights before. Jan hadn't been wrong about that. She had seen them continuously while she navigated the black labyrinth. She'd asked herself if they were part of the dead, but there was no way for her to know with any certainty and she had come to regard them as lights only, a mystery she might one day solve.

After Zoja was sure Jan was dead, she took hold of his frail body and dragged it out of the camp, down the luminescent path to the water. She left him on the edge of it so that Ozias could see him. He watched her carefully from inside his cage. He said nothing, not until she opened the door and released his shackles. He thanked her then, but she was already walking away, walking back to the camp.

She was sitting near the fire, waiting for him when he entered the camp. The pans Jan had used to cook with were on the ground, and he nudged them with his tattooed foot, then took a seat across from her.

'I owe you an explanation,' Ozias said once it became clear that Zoja wasn't going to speak first. 'I owe it to you more than anyone. I was born here in this labyrinth, in the black labyrinth, some time ago. I didn't lie to you about that. I don't know who my mother was, or my father. The monks raised me. They taught me how to read and write. They taught me about our faith. They taught me about the Black Queen. What they didn't know was that I already knew the Black Queen. She had been speaking to me since the day I was born. For a long time, I thought she spoke to all the children under her care, but it wasn't true. She spoke to me alone. She'd chosen me, she said. She had done it above all others. I was to give her freedom. The black monks were wary when I told them this. They'd begun to believe that the Black Queen was not as loyal to them as they were to her. They had reasons, but I was young and I didn't understand them. I only came to understand it once she was free, once she began destroying all that was around us.

'I had started to lose my faith before that. If I'm honest with you, I mean. It was the fault of the dead. The black labyrinth was full of the dead back then. They were on every street and in every building. Mostly they ignored you, and you ignored them, but I was different. I could talk to them. The Black Queen had given me that ability. The dead were to be my teachers. They were to teach me the languages and history and magick that I would need to free her. The dead knew that they were dead and thought of her as their enemy, but they were powerless to stop her demands. They didn't want to teach me but they couldn't stop themselves. The Black Queen had trapped them in a memory and they were forced to live the memory over and over. This was true of all the dead. You've probably seen it in the red labyrinth. According to the Black

Queen there was a child like me in the Red King's Labyrinth who was being taught in the same way. I was told she was a girl. A soulmate. A love. We were promised to each other. We were to be each other's reward. But she was murdered. She was killed by the red monks. They were rebelling against their god. That rebellion changed the Black Queen for me after that. Before, everything had gone the way she said. The dead would tell me that she wasn't a god but I didn't believe them. She was omniscient. She was everything. Now, through this failure, the dead were proved right and the Black Queen looked mortal. She looked trapped and frustrated. The world we were in was her failure. It was meant to be more than it was. It looked to me as if she had failed her creation and how could a god do that unless she herself was flawed.

'If the black monks had known about my doubt, they would have left me be. Maybe. But they didn't. They came to kill me. Their ranks were fractured though, and I was saved by those who remained loyal to the Black Queen. They helped hide me. I asked them why the Black Queen didn't strike down her enemies and they revealed to me that her power was tied to the black labyrinth. She was actually powerless, they said, because she was forced to maintain everything I saw around me. It was meant to awe me but only furthered my belief that she was not all powerful. When I turned eighteen, the monks took me to the Black Queen's throne room. She gave me the tattoos that you see on me now. They were the first complete map of the black labyrinth that anyone had ever seen. She gave them to me to protect me, she said. She gave it to me so that I would know where to go, where to hide, and where to cast the spells that would free her. I was nearing the end of my education then and the last stayed with me. Sometimes I wondered if it was not better to deny her, or to turn myself over to the other monks and let them kill me. It wouldn't have been hard. They were dangerous days for me, back then. There were traitors and assassination attempts every week. Sometimes it was too much for me. I would dream about the Red King's chosen one and how she waited for me. I knew she didn't, but I had no friends. I think that's why I eventually did what the Black Queen asked. She was all I had. She was my mother, lover, sister, and friend.

'I hated the violence that took place after I freed the Black Queen. She would sweep her hand and tear down dozens of buildings and roads. She ripped open the ground like it was nothing. She destroyed people. I saw it all while I stood at her side. The Black Queen told me I was her child. She promised me kingdoms and power and a wife who would adore me. I couldn't imagine it. I could only see the awful things she was doing. Eventually, it became too much and I fled. I fled to the Red King's kingdom, where I worked my way to the coast, to the great city that was there, the great city where you were, Zoja. I admit, I didn't plan on meeting you. My plan was to get some money and sail across the ocean and live in one of these other kingdoms. But then I met you. You who were so beautiful, who said the things I thought, who talked about the failures of this world in ways that I agreed. I fell in love with you though I should never have stayed. I should have just kept going. I knew the red monks were looking for me. They would find me eventually. But you were the first person I felt whole with. When Jan found me I knew I had not just failed myself, but you. I hated myself for putting you in danger. When they bought me back here I told myself I deserved it. Everything Jan did to me I accepted.

'But now I see that I was wrong to doubt the Black Queen. I was wrong to question my faith. The Black Queen told me she would honour her original words and find me a love like no other, and she has. I doubted her. I admit that. I didn't believe in her divine power. I didn't believe in her. But here you are. You were chosen by the Red King and because of that we make each other whole like no other couple in the world.'

11

SHE no longer called him Ozias. In the days after Zoja freed him, after he told her his story, she began to call him Eero. He preferred the name, he said. Zoja did as well, though for different reasons. Eero wanted to resume their relationship, but Zoja told him he was not the man she remembered and she couldn't return to what they'd once had. She had changed as well, she said. It was natural. Their lives had taken them to different places. They'd experienced different worlds. They had been changed by all that they'd seen and suffered. She didn't tell him that knowing he saw her presence here as reaffirmation not just of his faith in a false deity, but his love for her appalled her. She knew of nothing else that could have so cleanly severed her from the last, lingering feelings she had for Ozias. He was a stranger to her now, a stranger covered in black tattoos, a stranger who spoke quietly and assuredly about his falsehoods. Zoja responded and told him there were no gods and no designs. There was just power, raw and monstrous, and you made narratives to justify its exploitation of you.

Eero accepted that Zoja didn't share his faith, but he didn't respect it. In the following weeks and months he probed her lack of belief, explored it, tried to find ways to engage with it, but without luck. Zoja was not interested in talking to him about tenants of the Red King or the Black Queen, or the so-called tests he believed they had been subjected to. She left Jan's camp and made a place for herself in the debris of the black labyrinth. The luminescent light was pale there but she didn't mind. She made her bed out of rags and scavenged for a desk and what else she needed. She slept and studied there. She returned to the camp every second or third day to talk with Eero, to ask him questions, to borrow Jan's books. After a while, he accused her of not wanting to free the Red King because she refused to engage with him properly. Zoja shrugged and left him standing in the camp alone. It wasn't true, at any rate. Zoja never questioned what she was doing, not like I did. She was committed to her task. She had to be. She believed the Red King's changes within her were not all physical. The Red King could hear her words in the red labyrinth and while she thought he could not hear her in the black labyrinth, she believed she carried a part of him within her, like a parasite. If it did not talk to the Red King now, it would later when she met him again. The parasite, she believed, was in her mind, in her thoughts, and in the fragments of herself. He was in her fantasies, her dread, hope and the otherwise undefined parts of her. Zoja heard his words in her head, heard again how he'd spoken to her in the throne room, and knew that she could not show doubt or fear or hesitation otherwise the Red King would take it out later on those of us in the red labyrinth. The books she read and the lessons she had with Eero only highlighted her need to be careful. Magick was its own set of rules, Zoja discovered, its own language. Depending on what she did or didn't do, it obeyed, disobeyed, or constructed a new set of rules that she had to learn and adhere to, even if they contradicted the previous rules. With enough power, you could do almost anything, she realised, and the Red King had that power.

Zoja's relationship with Eero changed over time. It was only natural that it did. They felt around each other, fenced and sparred, but they were all each other had in the black labyrinth. They spent four years together. With each year that passed their relationship became more complex and difficult. They were a teacher and a student. They were old lovers. They were slaves. They were magicians. They were soldiers. They were chosen. They were forgotten. They were friends. They were enemies. Zoja struggled to keep their relationship distant and transactional. Eero struggled to renew their intimacy and to find forgiveness. Later, Zoja admitted to me that there were times when she saw Ozias and not Eero and she left her small, makeshift camp for his, or invited him into her own. These moments did not happen often and she was filled with regret after, but they did happen. They gave Eero a false hope and only fuelled his belief in the Black Queen's words. Zoja hated herself for it. She told herself that she had to leave, but Eero held back knowledge so that she couldn't. He could have taught her how to free the Red King early on in their time together, but he wanted her to love him and believed she was coming around to this, that she saw what he did about their future. After a while, Zoja took to using the magick she learned to fortify herself and her home. Towards the end of their time together, she said, Eero became desperate and difficult. She tried to be patient with him. She tried to be understanding. But Eero was not Ozias and he didn't understand that she could never forget that. Nor could she stand beside a man whose faith led him to believe that she was his reward for that lie and deception.

'I don't know that he ever really understood,' Zoja told me later, told me when we met again in the red labyrinth. 'Not even when I killed him.'

We were in the old dormitory when she said it. We were in the room we'd once shared, the room I lived in by myself now that Emy was dead and Signe had moved out. She'll come and find me if I'm there, Signe said on the day she left. We both knew it was a lie and we both pretended that it wasn't. Our problem was that we now reminded each other of things we'd rather forget. I'd managed to keep my room to myself partly because in the last few years the rate of new arrivals to the red labyrinth had declined. Tamasa said that it was because of the combination of the Black Queen's war and unrest among the monks.

A part of me wondered why Zoja told me about Eero. She didn't need to. I wouldn't have thought to ask. I'd been so surprised and delighted to see her when she returned that I might not have asked anything of her years away. I hardly recognised her. She had appeared at the dormitory's door wrapped in old robes. She was the figure you see now, lean and confident. Her hair had grown long. She didn't try to hide her tattoos. It would have been impossible, anyhow. They ran all over her maimed hand, got lost in her robes, and then reappeared on her neck, reaching up to her ear. She caught your eye when she talked. She held it. She commanded naturally and easily. She didn't need to tell me about Eero or why she had killed him because I was already loyal to her and her cause. It was only later that I realised much of what she told me wasn't for me alone. She was talking to the parasite in her, the Red King who could hear her now.

Zoja returned at the time our plans to escape reached their climax. We were ready. Nathaniel had dates and times, leaders and strike points. None of his plans involved Zoja. He hadn't expected her. None of us had, in fact. She'd been gone for so long that many of us had stopped hoping she would return. Some of us thought she was dead. Others said no, said that it would take her years to learn how to free the Red King, and we couldn't expect her in our lifetime. Tamasa thought that. She told me it, in fact. There was some concern among the others that she and her monks would try to stop us if we escaped, but I didn't believe it. Tamasa was fiercely loyal to the Red King and she did not care for her fellow monks, or for reason or consistency. She was mad herself. Many of the loyal monks were to greater or lesser degree. But such madness is hard to put your faith in. No one wanted to rely upon it, or trust it, not even me. The question of what Tamasa and her monks would do was like a scab Nathaniel and others picked at constantly. Zoja's return, then, was very welcome. Less welcome was her advice that we wait until she freed the Red King to begin our plans for escape.

'The chaos will help us,' she said.

'The chaos as he tears down the red labyrinth?'

'Yes.'

To free the Red King, Zoja explained, she had to travel throughout the red labyrinth, to seven points where seven magical seals lay. They were what tethered the Red King and his power to the red labyrinth, much like chains.

I was with Zoja when she broke open the first seal. It was not like what I thought it would be. Zoja took me to a random path not far from the dormitory, to the middle of a road, where we stood in the bloom of the lamps and watched the dead pass us.

'What's here today might not be here tomorrow,' Zoja said. 'One of the secrets of the red and black labyrinths is that they were always moving, always growing. Over time, I noticed it because my tattoos would change, because they'd have subtle shifts and would grow across my skin. The labyrinths were originally like twins in a womb, but the womb was the hollow of the earth. Now the black labyrinth is dead and no longer grows so the red is seeking to take its space. Eventually, it will fill all the black labyrinth had and then continue to fill the rest of the womb until it begins to break the surface of the earth apart.'

She took out a knife. There were runes etched along the blade, designs I'd never before seen. Zoja told me it was the knife she'd been given when she left the red labyrinth, but she'd altered it. She started to talk to herself in a language I didn't understand. It hurt my ears, though. I lifted my hands to muffle the sound as she pushed the knife forward. The blade disappeared as if it had pierced the world itself, as if the air was solid and could be cut. When she drew the knife back, fire fell to the ground like blood. I waited for more, but there was nothing. Zoja shook her knife, then put it away. I asked her if it was done and she assured me it was.

Tamasa told me the same thing later. She came to the dormitory to see me, but also to see Zoja, though the latter had already left. Tamasa sat on my bed and shared a meal with me.

'The Red King is pleased,' she said. 'You should prepare yourself for what will happen when he is released.'

'We've all been preparing.'

'You need to prepare yourself,' she said. 'There will be no law here after the seals are broken. There will only be chaos.'

'You won't try to keep the peace?'

'No.'

Later, I asked Jacek if he could get me a knife. I'd not carried a weapon in the red labyrinth. I had lived too long among the dead to send anyone to that fate. At least, that was what I thought before my own freedom came to be within reach.

Things got tense while Zoja made her way from seal to seal. It took about a month. She travelled by herself. She knew the red labyrinth better than any of us. She avoided patrols, slipped in and out of buildings, and very rarely used the new language she had learned. But the monks knew she was there. They heard the whispers. They saw the change in our behaviour. They raided dormitories trying to find her. They rounded up prisoners for questioning. Signe was one. The monks tortured those prisoners they took. We talked about rescue missions and retribution and I feared Nathaniel would lose control of everyone before Zoja was ready. But he didn't. He held us together. We were fraying and breaking but he held us until Zoja appeared before the Red King's throne.

The building stilled as she approached it. For days now, people had been talking about how it had slowed, how it was shifting less and less, but now, as Zoja walked up the road to it, it came to a complete stop. Its form was distorted, like its foundations had been disturbed during an earthquake, or an explosion had happened with it. A pair of monks emerged from it and approached Zoja. They were armed and armoured unlike any other monk in the red labyrinth, but rather than attack Zoja, they halted before her, bowed, and took up positions to guard her.

The last seal was here, hidden in a pocket of the universe. When Zoja pushed her knife into the world, the air around it began to burn. The bitter smell of it filled the red labyrinth. I smelt it at the restaurant. All of us did. We put down our trays and stopped our service. The dead continued despite this, continued in their loop of consumption. We left them and walked outside. I thought I could see fire in the air around the Red King's throne, but I realised I was wrong. There wasn't fire in the air, the air was on fire.

I turned to the others and told them that this was it, that we had to go now. I wasn't the only one who thought it. The Red King waited impatiently in his throne room. Zoja could see him through the distorted windows, could see his burning form in every pane of glass, in every flame in the air. He could taste his freedom and he was eager for it. Monks were rushing towards Zoja. She could hear her new guards fighting to protect her. Her knife was covered in flames. Her fingers were burning. She wanted to stop chanting. She wanted to release the knife. She wanted to close her eyes and wake up in the loft above her wig shop, having dreamed terribly. But she knew she couldn't. She was living in the real world, in this world of horrors. She was trapped in the red labyrinth with the dead and living and she would never be free if she released the knife. She gripped it hard and continued to chant—

And then it was done.

The Red King's throne melted into the air as if it had never existed. A void filled the space it had once occupied.

The Red King appeared on the road in front of Zoja. He appeared just as she had seen him before, an old, desiccated man covered in flames, wearing a crown of fire. The monks who had tried to stop Zoja, who had been fighting with her armoured guards, suddenly fell to their knees. They called out to the Red King in the language of the labyrinth and asked for forgiveness. Zoja didn't know why. She knew the Red King would not grant them mercy. She knew it before he waved his hand, before their heads ignited in cruel parodies of his own crown. The monks screamed. They tried to roll onto the ground, or to claw at their faces, but they couldn't. They couldn't because the Red King held them in their position, held them there so the flames would consume them, would devour their flesh, and then their bones while they still lived. It was punishment, but it was also the future. It was how the Red King would treat all his unfaithful monks. It was also how he would greet the prisoners he came in contact with, and with anyone else later. He would tear through the red labyrinth to reach his freedom and once he had it he would burn all those who lived in his cities, all those that had been loyal to his word and law as it had been reported to them. He would not care for them. He had never cared for them. He only cared for himself and one other. Now he was possessed of a fury that would not be consumed by a few deaths. It would only be sated once millions were dead. He would not be finished even when all the fields he saw were burning and all were filled with smouldering bones, just as the Black Queen had not been. With their insatiable need for revenge and domination, the two of them would reunite and continue their destruction across the ocean. They would lay wake to the world they believed was their own, the world they would later rebuild in their own distorted vision of perfection.

Zoja saw this.

She saw it in a moment, saw a whole eternity spent under the rule of a new tyranny, saw it as the Red King began to walk past her.

Zoja drove her knife into his chest. If he saw her thought before it took place, if the thought she had buried deep within herself for years gave itself shape, if he realised her intention before the blade pierced his skin, it was not with enough time to stop the blow, or to prevent the twist of the blade that followed. Zoja started to chant as she drove her knife into him again. Her chant changed, became what sounded like one stretched out scream, full of power. The air around her sparked, sparked and burst, but did not catch alight.

The Red King fell backwards. 'I'll not break one prison only for you to make another,' Zoja whispered to him while he lay on the ground. The Red King tried to speak but he couldn't find the words or the breath or the intent to form the words aloud or within Zoja's head. The loyal guards rushed towards her, but the ground beneath them sparked and suddenly gave away. 'I'll kill my gods, my kings, and my masters before I'll make another cage.' The fire around the Red King was dying, the life in his eyes following it. 'I'll kill your queen next,' Zoja said, and maybe he heard those words, maybe not.

There are some who tell you that this is not how the Red King died. There are some who will say that there was a great battle between Zoja and the Red King, that their magick tore apart the red labyrinth, and that they killed hundreds while fighting. I have heard stories that this battle came with eclipses, with the sudden extinguishing of all the lights in the red labyrinth, with earthquakes in the mountains and tidal waves that swamped the Red King's city. I have heard even that the Black Queen screamed from the depth of her kingdom, screamed so loudly that it could be heard within the red labyrinth itself, that we all felt it in our hearts because a god's loss is the only true loss the world will ever know. But it's not true. None of it is true. You know that because there were no tidal waves here. I know because I was there. What is true is that Zoja struck the Red King with her knife. She did it while his attention was elsewhere. Zoja told me this and she will tell you this if you come with me, if you wish to ask her yourself. She will tell you because she is the only one who was there when the Red King died.

There was chaos after. I can tell you that easily. There was chaos before, in fact. But when the red labyrinth began to break apart because the Red King's power no longer coursed through it, when the earth started to fall in on us and roads broke and gave way, the chaos got worse. For a while no one knew what they were doing. They were terrified. They sunk to their knees. They held each other. They fought. Pandemonium reigned.

The dead gained their freedom as well. There are few things I will be able to forget about my escape from the red labyrinth, but I wish I could forget the dead and the moment when they were suddenly aware of what they were doing, or just how cruelly they'd been kept. Then, after that shock, came a further awareness of what awaited them now. Oblivion awaited. For some you could see that such a thought was a pleasure, but for others, it was not. The terrified dead ran for the living, for the prisoner and the monk alike, trying to grab us, to possess us, to live again through theft, only to dissolve into the air and be replaced by another of the dead who was terrified, confused, or happy. Generations of generations of dead came to themselves as the red labyrinth began to break apart. This awareness was not limited to those like you and I, either. Dead animals ran at us, or huddled in corners, or howled silently. Some of the dead searched for others. Some tried to speak to you. Some made gestures. Then, in a handful of heartbeats, in a moment that stretched forever and that still lives in me with a clarity I wish it did not, the dead were gone.

Nothing that followed was simple, or orderly. The red labyrinth shook. Some monks tried to restore order. We resisted. We wouldn't go back to our dormitories. We wouldn't await for the red labyrinth to fall in on us. We fought. We could hear the earth begin to break. I don't think any of us would have escaped if not for Nathaniel and his plans. He restored order. He made us follow the plans he had laid out earlier. He issued simple orders. Jacek went to rescue the prisoners like Signe who had been taken. He found them battered and tortured and did his best to move them towards the exits. I took my command and pushed forward to help him. I saw Signe fall before the doors that led out. By the time I reached her, she was already gone. I killed Tamasa soon after. I who had never killed anyone killed her first. She knew our plans. She waited for us in the stairwell with her loyalists, armed with crossbows and swords. It was an awful fight, bloody and unnecessary. As she lay dying, I sat beside her and held her hand. My knife was in her chest and she was bleeding out. She kept talking about the Red King. The Black Queen would come for us, would come for revenge. She will come for you, my love, she said while we bought in the battering rams we had made, the rams we would use to break the stone doors down with and push up the shaking stairs to the monastery and freedom. She will come for you, she whispered again. Be careful, be careful.

After she died, I took my knife back. I took it back and returned to the red labyrinth, to the fighting that was taking place, to Zoja who was doing her best to hold what she could of it together so that we could use the roads and escape. I went back to make sure no one was left behind, that no more of us were fed to the madness within it.

12

WE came out into the monastery battered and desperate. I came out with Zoja. We were the last to leave the red labyrinth. The passages crumbled as we came out of them. There were red monks in there and maybe they are still there, digging themselves out, or eating the remains of themselves and their god. I don't know. I don't care.

We came out into the night, into a clear dark night full of stars. We were shocked because most of us thought it was day. We laughed a little. We scouted the grounds and saw to our injured. The monks who lived in the monastery had fled. They had left their crops, their livestock, and their wards behind. We found the children locked in their rooms. Many of the monks who fled went to the Red King's city, went to the council, to the leaders they knew and trusted. Some went further. Some sought out the Black Queen and her loyalists. It is said that she knew the Red King was dead and that she wept tears of black blood and vowed vengeance. The red monks who went to her changed their colours and, in the months that followed, they came back into our lands with her loyalists. The war that had been taking place a decade ago when Jacek was imprisoned was over now. The Black Queen's representatives met no resistance. In fact, they found allies in the councils who don't want to give up their power, in the so called faithful of the Red King who were only happy to become the Black Queen's faithful if they could keep their positions. In her name, they have since raised taxes and bled all around you dry. The ships that now arrive at your docks are full of mercenaries the Black Queen has bought with your money. They cross the border into her land because she hasn't yet left. She is reluctant to come into what was once her husband's kingdom. One day she will, however. She still holds to her dream. She still believes the world is hers to remake.

Zoja has fortified herself in the mountains. We live in the monastery that sits above the remains of the red labyrinth. We live in the mountains that surround it, the mountains that lead to the entrance of the black labyrinth. They are ours now. We prepare ourselves for war with the Black Queen, but we also teach those who come to us how to read, the history that has been kept from them, and magick. Zoja will not hoard her knowledge. She will not use it to lift herself above you or anyone else. She has no interest in that. We live in a community. We serve each other. We protect each other. We ensure our equality. We will not repeat the mistakes we were raised in, that we lived in. We will not recreate the conditions that gave rise to our suffering, or to yours.

I am one of the people who leave the mountains and come down to the towns and cities to tell you what has happened. It is dangerous, but I do it. I do it because everywhere I go, I see people like you, people who are struggling to feed your families and yourself. I know many of you lost your siblings and parents to war years ago and now find your children and partners conscripted to a new one that sounds much worse. I know the prefects raid your businesses and your houses in search of spies and dissidents. I know you are afraid to speak. I know because this happens everywhere now. We live in fear. We live in cages with no bars. I come here and I speak to you because I will not pretend that it doesn't exist, or that it is unknown to me. I lived in the red labyrinth for over thirty years, and it took my youth and my children and my future, and I see the same thing happening here to you.

You don't have to come with me. I don't ask that of you, though you are free to do so. You don't have to follow me, or Zoja Rose. Like I said earlier, Zoja does not care if you support her or not. She only cares that you know the truth of what has happened. She wants you to know that you've been lied to and that you do not need false gods, or kings and queens who think themselves better than us. She wants you to know that you need no masters. She will tell you that if you come with me, just as I have told you. She will tell you that the only way to treat someone who claims to rule you is to take a knife to them.

A PARTIAL LIST OF SNUGGLY BOOKS

G. ALBERT AURIER *Elsewhere and Other Stories*
CHARLES BARBARA *My Lunatic Asylum*
S. HEZOLNRY BERTHOUD *Misanthropic Tales*
LÉON BLOY *The Tarantulas' Parlor and Other Unkind Tales*
ÉLÉMIR BOURGES *The Twilight of the Gods*
CYRIEL BUYSSE *The Aunts*
JAMES CHAMPAGNE *Harlem Smoke*
FÉLICIEN CHAMPSAUR *The Latin Orgy*
BRENDAN CONNELL *Metrophilias*
BRENDAN CONNELL *Spells*
BRENDAN CONNELL (editor)
    The World in Violet: An Anthology of EnglishDecadent Poetry
RAFAELA CONTRERAS *The Turquoise Ring and Other Stories*
DANIEL CORRICK (editor)
    Ghosts and Robbers: An Anthology of German Gothic Fiction
ADOLFO COUVE *When I Think of My Missing Head*
QUENTIN S. CRISP *Aiaigasa*
LUCIE DELARUE-MARDRUS *The Last Siren and Other Stories*
LADY DILKE *The Outcast Spirit and Other Stories*
CATHERINE DOUSTEYSSIER-KHOZE *The Beauty of the Death Cap*
ÉDOUARD DUJARDIN *Hauntings*
BERIT ELLINGSEN *Now We Can See the Moon*
ERCKMANN-CHATRIAN *A Malediction*
ALPHONSE ESQUIROS *The Enchanted Castle*
ENRIQUE GÓMEZ CARRILLO *Sentimental Stories*
DELPHI FABRICE *Flowers of Ether*
DELPHI FABRICE *The Red Sorcerer*
DELPHI FABRICE *The Red Spider*
BENJAMIN GASTINEAU *The Reign of Satan*
EDMOND AND JULES DE GONCOURT *Manette Salomon*
REMY DE GOURMONT *From a Faraway Land*
REMY DE GOURMONT *Morose Vignettes*
GUIDO GOZZANO *Alcina and Other Stories*
GUSTAVE GUICHES *The Modesty of Sodom*
EDWARD HERON-ALLEN *The Complete Shorter Fiction*
EDWARD HERON-ALLEN *Three Ghost-Written Novels*
J.-K. HUYSMANS *The Crowds of Lourdes*
J.-K. HUYSMANS *Knapsacks*
COLIN INSOLE *Valerie and Other Stories*
JUSTIN ISIS *Pleasant Tales II*

JULES JANIN *The Dead Donkey and the Guillotined Woman*
VICTOR JOLY *The Unknown Collaborator and Other Legendary Tales*
GUSTAVE KAHN *The Mad King*
MARIE KRYSINSKA *The Path of Amour*
BERNARD LAZARE *The Mirror of Legends*
BERNARD LAZARE *The Torch-Bearers*
MAURICE LEVEL *The Shadow*
JEAN LORRAIN *Errant Vice*
JEAN LORRAIN *Fards and Poisons*
JEAN LORRAIN *Masks in the Tapestry*
JEAN LORRAIN *Monsieur de Bougrelon and Other Stories*
JEAN LORRAIN *Nightmares of an Ether-Drinker*
JEAN LORRAIN *The Soul-Drinker and Other Decadent Fantasies*
GEORGES DE LYS *An Idyll in Sodom*
GEORGES DE LYS *Penthesilea*
ARTHUR MACHEN *N*
ARTHUR MACHEN *Ornaments in Jade*
CAMILLE MAUCLAIR *The Frail Soul and Other Stories*
CATULLE MENDÈS *Bluebirds*
CATULLE MENDÈS *For Reading in the Bath*
CATULLE MENDÈS *Mephistophela*
ÉPHRAÏM MIKHAËL *Halyartes and Other Poems in Prose*
LUIS DE MIRANDA *Who Killed the Poet?*
OCTAVE MIRBEAU *The Death of Balzac*
CHARLES MORICE *Babels, Balloons and Innocent Eyes*
GABRIEL MOUREY *Monada*
DAMIAN MURPHY *Daughters of Apostasy*
KRISTINE ONG MUSLIM *Butterfly Dream*
OSSIT *Ilse*
CHARLES NODIER *Outlaws and Sorrows*
HERSH DOVID NOMBERG *A Cheerful Soul and Other Stories*
PHILOTHÉE O'NEDDY *The Enchanted Ring*
GEORGES DE PEYREBRUNE *A Decadent Woman*
HÉLÈNE PICARD *Sabbat*
URSULA PFLUG *Down From*
JEAN PRINTEMPS *Whimsical Tales*
RACHILDE *The Princess of Darkness*
JEREMY REED *When a Girl Loves a Girl*
ADOLPHE RETTÉ *Misty Thule*
JEAN RICHEPIN *The Bull-Man and the Grasshopper*
FREDERICK ROLFE (Baron Corvo) *Amico di Sandro*
FREDERICK ROLFE (Baron Corvo) *An Ossuary of the North Lagoon and Other Stories*

JASON ROLFE *An Archive of Human Nonsense*
ARNAUD RYKNER *The Last Train*
LEOPOLD VON SACHER-MASOCH
    The Black Gondola and Other Stories
MARCEL SCHWOB *The Assassins and Other Stories*
MARCEL SCHWOB *Double Heart*
CHRISTIAN HEINRICH SPIESS *The Dwarf of Westerbourg*
BRIAN STABLEFORD (editor)
    Decadence and Symbolism: A Showcase Anthology
BRIAN STABLEFORD (editor) *The Snuggly Satyricon*
BRIAN STABLEFORD (editor) *The Snuggly Satanicon*
BRIAN STABLEFORD *Spirits of the Vasty Deep*
COUNT ERIC STENBOCK *Love, Sleep & Dreams*
COUNT ERIC STENBOCK *Myrtle, Rue & Cypress*
COUNT ERIC STENBOCK *The Shadow of Death*
COUNT ERIC STENBOCK *Studies of Death*
MONTAGUE SUMMERS *The Bride of Christ and Other Fictions*
MONTAGUE SUMMERS *Six Ghost Stories*
ALICE TÉLOT *The Inn of Tears*
GILBERT-AUGUSTIN THIERRY *The Blonde Tress and The Mask*
GILBERT-AUGUSTIN THIERRY *Reincarnation and Redemption*
DOUGLAS THOMPSON *The Fallen West*
TOADHOUSE *Gone Fishing with Samy Rosenstock*
TOADHOUSE *Living and Dying in a Mind Field*
TOADHOUSE *What Makes the Wave Break?*
LÉO TRÉZENIK *The Confession of a Madman*
LÉO TRÉZENIK *Decadent Prose Pieces*
RUGGERO VASARI *Raun*
ILARIE VORONCA *The Confession of a False Soul*
ILARIE VORONCA *The Key to Reality*
JANE DE LA VAUDÈRE *The Demi-Sexes and The Androgynes*
JANE DE LA VAUDÈRE *The Double Star and Other Occult Fantasies*
AUGUSTE VILLIERS DE L'ISLE-ADAM *Isis*
RENÉE VIVIEN AND HÉLÈNE DE ZUYLEN DE NYEVELT
    Faustina and Other Stories
RENÉE VIVIEN *Lilith's Legacy*
RENÉE VIVIEN *A Woman Appeared to Me*
ILARIE VORONCA *The Confession of a False Soul*
ILARIE VORONCA *The Key to Reality*
TERESA WILMS MONTT *In the Stillness of Marble*
TERESA WILMS MONTT *S^entimental Doubts*
KAREL VAN DE WOESTIJNE *The Dying Peasant*

www.ingramcontent.com/pod-product-compliance
Ingram Content Group UK Ltd.
Pitfield, Milton Keynes, MK11 3LW, UK
UKHW011419050625
6261UKWH00025B/278